CARSON McCULLERS (1917-1967)

When she was only twenty-three, Carson Mc-Cullers' first novel, The Heart Is a Lonely Hunter, *became a literary sensation. Since that time, her reputation has grown with every successive work.*

Such novels as Reflections in a Golden Eye, The Member of the Wedding *and* Clock Without Hands *have won her comparison with such diverse masters as Melville, Flaubert and Faulkner —which is to say: no critic has succeeded in easily capsulizing the full dimensions of her talent.*

Perhaps none of her works more brilliantly represents the variety and richness of her art than The Ballad of the Sad Café. *In the already classic novella of the title, and in the tales which accompany it, the genius of Carson McCullers shines forth vividly—and unforgettably.*

BANTAM MODERN CLASSICS
Ask your bookseller for the books you have missed

THE BALLAD OF THE SAD CAFÉ
and Other Stories

CARSON McCULLERS

BANTAM BOOKS · TORONTO · NEW YORK · LONDON

THE BALLAD OF THE SAD CAFÉ
AND OTHER STORIES

*A Bantam Book / published by arrangement with
Houghton Mifflin Company*

PRINTING HISTORY
Houghton Mifflin edition published May 1951
2nd printing .... December 1958

Book Find Club edition published May 1951

2nd printing .... May 1952	4th printing .... April 1953
3rd printing .... January 1953	5th printing .... June 1954

Bantam edition published March 1958

2nd printing .... May 1962	6th printing ...... January 1966
3rd printing .... July 1962	7th printing ... November 1966
4th printing .... June 1964	8th printing ..... October 1967
5th printing .... July 1965	9th printing .... February 1968

Bantam Modern Classic edition published August 1969

11th printing
12th printing
13th printing

The works in this volume are selected and reprinted from
The Ballad of the Sad Café, *published by Houghton Mifflin Company, May 1951.*
"The Ballad of the Sad Café" *and* "A Tree, A Rock, A Cloud" *originally appeared in* HARPER'S BAZAAR; "The Jockey" *and* "Madame Zilensky and the King of Finland" *in* THE NEW YORKER; "Wunderkind" *in* STORY MAGAZINE; "The Sojourner" *in* MADEMOISELLE.
"A Domestic Dilemma" *and* "The Sojourner" *appeared in the* New York POST, 1951.

Bantam Books are published by Bantam Books, Inc., a subsidiary of Grosset & Dunlap, Inc. Its trade-mark, consisting of the words "Bantam Books" and the portrayal of a bantam, is registered in the United States Patent Office and in other countries. Marca Registrada. Bantam Books, Inc., 271 Madison Avenue, New York, N.Y. 10016.

PRINTED IN THE UNITED STATES OF AMERICA

CONTENTS

The Ballad of
the Sad Café

The Ballad of the Sad Café

THE TOWN itself is dreary; not much is there except the cotton mill, the two-room houses where the workers live, a few peach trees, a church with two colored windows, and a miserable main street only a hundred yards long. On Saturdays the tenants from the near-by farms come in for a day of talk and trade. Otherwise the town is lonesome, sad, and like a place that is far off and estranged from all other places in the world. The nearest train stop is Society City, and the Greyhound and White Bus Lines use the Forks Falls Road which is three miles away. The winters here are short and raw, the summers white with glare and fiery hot.

If you walk along the main street on an August afternoon there is nothing whatsoever to do. The largest building, in the very center of the town, is boarded up completely and leans so far to the right that it seems bound to collapse at any minute. The house is very old. There is about it a curious, cracked look that is very puzzling until you suddenly realize that at one time, and long ago, the right side of the front porch had been painted, and part of the wall—but the painting was left unfinished and one portion of the house is darker and dingier than the other. The building looks completely deserted. Nevertheless, on the second floor there is one window which is not boarded; sometimes in the late afternoon when the heat is at its worst a hand will slowly open the shutter and a face will look down on the town. It is a face like the terrible dim faces known in dreams— sexless and white, with two gray crossed eyes which are

3

turned inward so sharply that they seem to be exchanging with each other one long and secret gaze of grief. The face lingers at the window for an hour or so, then the shutters are closed once more, and as likely as not there will not be another soul to be seen along the main street. These August afternoons—when your shift is finished there is absolutely nothing to do; you might as well walk down to the Forks Falls Road and listen to the chain gang.

However, here in this very town there was once a café. And this old boarded-up house was unlike any other place for many miles around. There were tables with cloths and paper napkins, colored streamers from the electric fans, great gatherings on Saturday nights. The owner of the place was Miss Amelia Evans. But the person most responsible for the success and gaiety of the place was a hunchback called Cousin Lymon. One other person had a part in the story of this café—he was the former husband of Miss Amelia, a terrible character who returned to the town after a long term in the penitentiary, caused ruin, and then went on his way again. The café has long since been closed, but it is still remembered.

The place was not always a café. Miss Amelia inherited the building from her father, and it was a store that carried mostly feed, guano, and staples such as meal and snuff. Miss Amelia was rich. In addition to the store she operated a still three miles back in the swamp, and ran out the best liquor in the county. She was a dark, tall woman with bones and muscles like a man. Her hair was cut short and brushed back from the forehead, and there was about her sunburned face a tense, haggard quality. She might have been a handsome woman if, even then, she was not slightly cross-eyed. There were those who would have courted her, but Miss Amelia cared nothing for the love of men and was a solitary person. Her marriage had been unlike any other marriage ever contracted in this county—it was a strange and dangerous marriage, lasting only for ten days, that left the whole town wondering and shocked. Except for this queer marriage, Miss Amelia had lived her life alone. Often she spent whole nights back in her shed in the swamp, dressed in overalls and gum boots, silently guarding the low fire of the still.

With all things which could be made by the hands Miss Amelia prospered. She sold chitterlins and sausage in the town near-by. On fine autumn days, she ground sorghum, and the syrup from her vats was dark golden and delicately flavored. She built the brick privy behind her store in only two weeks and was skilled in carpentering. It was only with people that Miss Amelia was not at ease. People, unless they are nilly-willy or very sick, cannot be taken into the hands and changed overnight to something more worthwhile and profitable. So that the only use that Miss Amelia had for other people was to make money out of them. And in this she succeeded. Mortgages on crops and property, a sawmill, money in the bank—she was the richest woman for miles around. She would have been rich as a congressman if it were not for her one great failing, and that was her passion for lawsuits and the courts. She would involve herself in long and bitter litigation over just a trifle. It was said that if Miss Amelia so much as stumbled over a rock in the road she would glance around instinctively as though looking for something to sue about it. Aside from these lawsuits she lived a steady life and every day was very much like the day that had gone before. With the exception of her ten-day marriage, nothing happened to change this until the spring of the year that Miss Amelia was thirty years old.

It was toward midnight on a soft quiet evening in April. The sky was the color of a blue swamp iris, the moon clear and bright. The crops that spring promised well and in the past weeks the mill had run a night shift. Down by the creek the square brick factory was yellow with light, and there was the faint, steady hum of the looms. It was such a night when it is good to hear from faraway, across the dark fields, the slow song of a Negro on his way to make love. Or when it is pleasant

5

to sit quietly and pick a guitar, or simply to rest alone and think of nothing at all. The street that evening was deserted, but Miss Amelia's store was lighted and on the porch outside there were five people. One of these was Stumpy MacPhail, a foreman with a red face and dainty, purplish hands. On the top step were two boys in overalls, the Rainey twins—both of them lanky and slow, with white hair and sleepy green eyes. The other man was Henry Macy, a shy and timid person with gentle manners and nervous ways, who sat on the edge of the bottom step. Miss Amelia herself stood leaning against the side of the open door, her feet crossed in their big swamp boots, patiently untying knots in a rope she had come across. They had not talked for a long time.

One of the twins, who had been looking down the empty road, was the first to speak. 'I see something coming,' he said.

'A calf got loose,' said his brother.

The approaching figure was still too distant to be clearly seen. The moon made dim, twisted shadows of the blossoming peach trees along the side of the road. In the air the odor of blossoms and sweet spring grass mingled with the warm, sour smell of the near-by lagoon.

'No. It's somebody's youngun,' said Stumpy MacPhail.

Miss Amelia watched the road in silence. She had put down her rope and was fingering the straps of her overalls with her brown bony hand. She scowled, and a dark lock of hair fell down on her forehead. While they were waiting there, a dog from one of the houses down the road began a wild, hoarse howl that continued until a voice called out and hushed him. It was not until the figure was quite close, within the range of the yellow light from the porch, that they saw clearly what had come.

The man was a stranger, and it is rare that a stranger enters the town on foot at that hour. Besides, the man was a hunchback. He was scarcely more than four feet tall and he wore a ragged, dusty coat that reached only to his knees. His crooked little legs seemed too thin to carry the weight of his great warped chest and the hump that sat on his shoulders. He had a very large head, with deep-set blue eyes and a sharp little mouth. His face was both soft and sassy—at the moment his pale skin was yellowed by dust and there were lavendar shadows beneath his eyes. He carried a lopsided old suitcase which was tied with a rope.

'Evening,' said the hunchback, and he was out of breath.

Miss Amelia and the men on the porch neither answered his greeting nor spoke. They only looked at him.

'I am hunting for Miss Amelia Evans.'

Miss Amelia pushed back her hair from her forehead and raised her chin. 'How come?'

'Because I am kin to her,' the hunchback said.

The twins and Stumpy MacPhail looked up at Miss Amelia.

'That's me,' she said. 'How do you mean "kin"?'

'Because——' the hunchback began. He looked uneasy, almost as though he was about to cry. He rested the suitcase on the bottom step, but did not take his hand from the handle. 'My mother was Fanny Jesup and she come from Cheehaw. She left Cheehaw some thirty years ago when she married her first husband. I remember hearing her tell how she had a half-sister named Martha. And back in Cheehaw today they tell me that was your mother.'

Miss Amelia listened with her head turned slightly aside. She ate her Sunday dinners by herself; her place was never crowded with a flock of relatives, and she claimed kin with no one. She had had a great-aunt who owned the livery stable in Cheehaw, but that aunt was now dead. Aside from her there was only one double first cousin who lived in a town twenty miles away, but this cousin and Miss Amelia did not get on so well, and when they chanced to pass each other they spat on the side of the road. Other people had tried very hard, from time to time, to work out some kind of far-fetched connection with Miss Amelia, but with absolutely no success.

The hunchback went into a long rigmarole, mentioning names and places that were unknown to the listeners on the porch and seemed to have nothing to do with the subject. 'So Fanny and Martha Jesup were half-sisters. And I am the son of Fanny's third husband. So that would make you and I——' He bent down and began to unfasten his suitcase. His hands were like dirty sparrow claws and they were trembling. The bag was full of all manner of junk—ragged clothes and odd rubbish that looked like parts out of a sewing machine, or something just as worthless. The hunchback scrambled among these belongings and brought out an old photograph. 'This is a picture of my mother and her half-sister.'

Miss Amelia did not speak. She was moving her jaw slowly from side to side, and you could tell from her face what she was thinking about. Stumpy MacPhail took the photograph and held it out toward the light. It was a picture of two pale, withered-up little children of about two and three years of age. The faces were tiny white blurs, and it might have been an old picture in anyone's album.

Stumpy MacPhail handed it back with no comment. 'Where you come from?' he asked.

The hunchback's voice was uncertain. 'I was traveling.'

Still Miss Amelia did not speak. She just stood leaning against the side of the door, and looked down at the hunchback. Henry Macy winked nervously and rubbed his hands together. Then quietly he left the bottom step and disappeared. He is a good soul, and the hunchback's situation had touched his heart. Therefore he did not want to wait and watch Miss Amelia chase this newcomer off her property and run him out of town. The hunchback stood with his bag open on the bottom step; he sniffled his nose, and his mouth quivered. Perhaps he began to feel his dismal predicament. Maybe he realized what a miserable thing it was to be a stranger in the town with a suitcase full of junk, and claiming kin with Miss Amelia. At any rate he sat down on the steps and suddenly began to cry.

It was not a common thing to have an unknown hunchback walk to the store at midnight and then sit down and cry. Miss Amelia rubbed back her hair from her forehead and the men looked at each other uncomfortably. All around the town was very quiet.

At last one of the twins said: 'I'll be damned if he ain't a regular Morris Finestein.'

Everyone nodded and agreed, for that is an expression having a certain special meaning. But the hunchback cried louder because he could not know what they were talking about. Morris Finestein was a person who had lived in the town years before. He was only a quick, skipping little Jew who cried if you called him Christ-killer, and ate light bread and canned salmon every day. A calamity had come over him and he had moved away to Society City. But since then if a man were prissy in any way, or if a man ever wept, he was known as a Morris Finestein.

'Well, he is afflicted,' said Stumpy MacPhail. 'There is some cause.'

Miss Amelia crossed the porch with two slow, gangling strides. She went down the steps and stood looking thoughtfully at the stranger. Gingerly, with one long brown forefinger, she touched the hump on his back. The hunchback still wept, but he was quieter now. The night was silent and the moon still shone with a soft, clear light—it was getting colder. Then Miss Amelia did a rare thing; she pulled out a bottle from her hip pocket and after polishing off the top with the palm of her hand she handed it to the hunchback to drink. Miss Amelia could seldom be persuaded to sell her liquor on credit, and for her to give so much as a drop away free was almost unknown.

'Drink,' she said. 'It will liven your gizzard.'

The hunchback stopped crying, neatly licked the tears

from around his mouth, and did as he was told. When he was finished, Miss Amelia took a slow swallow, warmed and washed her mouth with it, and spat. Then she also drank. The twins and the foreman had their own bottle they had paid for.

'It is smooth liquor,' Stumpy MacPhail said. 'Miss Amelia, I have never known you to fail.'

The whisky they drank that evening (two big bottles of it) is important. Otherwise, it would be hard to account for what followed. Perhaps without it there would never have been a café. For the liquor of Miss Amelia has a special quality of its own. It is clean and sharp on the tongue, but once down a man it glows inside him for a long time afterward. And that is not all. It is known that if a message is written with lemon juice on a clean sheet of paper there will be no sign of it. But if the paper is held for a moment to the fire then the letters turn brown and the meaning becomes clear. Imagine that the whisky is the fire and that the message is that which is known only in the soul of a man—then the worth of Miss Amelia's liquor can be understood. Things that have gone unnoticed, thoughts that have been harbored far back in the dark mind, are suddenly recognized and comprehended. A spinner who has thought only of the loom, the dinner pail, the bed, and then the loom again—this spinner might drink some on a Sunday and come across a marsh lily. And in his palm he might hold this flower, examining the golden dainty cup, and in him suddenly might come a sweetness keen as pain. A weaver might look up suddenly and see for the first time the cold, weird radiance of midnight January sky, and a deep fright at his own smallness stop his heart. Such things as these, then, happen when a man has drunk Miss Amelia's liquor. He may suffer, or he may be spent with joy—but the experience has shown the truth; he has warmed his soul and seen the message hidden there.

They drank until it was past midnight, and the moon

was clouded over so that the night was cold and dark. The hunchback still sat on the bottom steps, bent over miserably with his forehead resting on his knee. Miss Amelia stood with her hands in her pockets, one foot resting on the second step of the stairs. She had been silent for a long time. Her face had the expression often seen in slightly cross-eyed persons who are thinking deeply, a look that appears to be both very wise and very crazy. At last she said: 'I don't know your name.'

'I'm Lymon Willis,' said the hunchback.

'Well, come on in,' she said. 'Some supper was left in the stove and you can eat.'

Only a few times in her life had Miss Amelia invited anyone to eat with her, unless she were planning to trick them in some way, or make money out of them. So the men on the porch felt there was something wrong. Later, they said among themselves that she must have been drinking back in the swamp the better part of the afternoon. At any rate she left the porch, and Stumpy MacPhail and the twins went on off home. She bolted the front door and looked all around to see that her goods were in order. Then she went to the kitchen, which was at the back of the store. The hunchback followed her, dragging his suitcase, sniffing and wiping his nose on the sleeve of his dirty coat.

'Sit down,' said Miss Amelia. 'I'll just warm up what's here.'

It was a good meal they had together on that night. Miss Amelia was rich and she did not grudge herself food. There was fried chicken (the breast of which the hunchback took on his own plate), mashed rootabeggars, collard greens, and hot, pale golden, sweet potatoes. Miss Amelia ate slowly and with the relish of a farm hand. She sat with both elbows on the table, bent over the plate, her knees spread wide apart and her feet braced on the rungs of the chair. As for the hunchback, he gulped down his supper as though he had not smelled food in months. During the meal one tear crept down his dingy cheek—but it was just a little leftover tear

11

and meant nothing at all. The lamp on the table was well-trimmed, burning blue at the edges of the wick, and casting a cheerful light in the kitchen. When Miss Amelia had eaten her supper she wiped her plate carefully with a slice of light bread, and then poured her own clear, sweet syrup over the bread. The hunchback did likewise—except that he was more finicky and asked for a new plate. Having finished, Miss Amelia tilted back her chair, tightened her fist, and felt the hard, supple muscles of her right arm beneath the clean, blue cloth of her shirtsleeves—an unconscious habit with her, at the close of a meal. Then she took the lamp from the table and jerked her head toward the staircase as an invitation for the hunchback to follow after her.

Above the store there were the three rooms where Miss Amelia had lived during all her life—two bedrooms with a large parlor in between. Few people had even seen these rooms, but it was generally known that they were well-furnished and extremely clean. And now Miss Amelia was taking up with her a dirty little hunchbacked stranger, come from God knows where. Miss Amelia walked slowly, two steps at a time, holding the lamp high. The hunchback hovered so close behind her that the swinging light made on the staircase wall one great, twisted shadow of the two of them. Soon the premises above the store were dark as the rest of the town.

The next morning was serene, with a sunrise of warm purple mixed with rose. In the fields around the town the furrows were newly plowed, and very early the tenants were at work setting out the young, deep green tobacco plants. The wild crows flew down close to the fields, making swift blue shadows on the earth. In town the people set out early with their dinner pails, and the windows of the mill were blinding gold in the sun. The air was fresh and the peach trees light as March clouds with their blossoms.

Miss Amelia came down at about dawn, as usual. She

washed her head at the pump and very shortly set about her business. Later in the morning she saddled her mule and went to see about her property, planted with cotton, up near the Forks Falls Road. By noon, of course, everybody had heard about the hunchback who had come to the store in the middle of the night. But no one as yet had seen him. The day soon grew hot and the sky was a rich, midday blue. Still no one had laid an eye on this strange guest. A few people remembered that Miss Amelia's mother had had a half-sister—but there was some difference of opinion as to whether she had died or had run off with a tobacco stringer. As for the hunchback's claim, everyone thought it was a trumped-up business. And the town, knowing Miss Amelia, decided that surely she had put him out of the house after feeding him. But toward evening, when the sky had whitened, and the shift was done, a woman claimed to have seen a crooked face at the window of one of the rooms up over the store. Miss Amelia herself said nothing. She clerked in the store for a while, argued for an hour with a farmer over a plow shaft, mended some chicken wire, locked up near sundown, and went to her rooms. The town was left puzzled and talkative.

The next day Miss Amelia did not open the store, but stayed locked up inside her premises and saw no one. Now this was the day that the rumor started—the rumor so terrible that the town and all the country about were stunned by it. The rumor was started by a weaver called Merlie Ryan. He is a man of not much account—sallow, shambling, and with no teeth in his head. He has the three-day malaria, which means that every third day the fever comes on him. So on two days he is dull and cross, but on the third day he livens up and sometimes has an idea or two, most of which are foolish. It was while Merlie Ryan was in his fever that he turned suddenly and said:

'I know what Miss Amelia done. She murdered that man for something in that suitcase.'

He said this in a calm voice, as a statement of fact.

13

And within an hour the news had swept through the town. It was a fierce and sickly tale the town built up that day. In it were all the things which cause the heart to shiver—a hunchback, a midnight burial in the swamp, the dragging of Miss Amelia through the streets of the town on the way to prison, the squabbles over what would happen to her property—all told in hushed voices and repeated with some fresh and weird detail. It rained and women forgot to bring in the washing from the lines. One or two mortals, who were in debt to Miss Amelia, even put on Sunday clothes as though it were a holiday. People clustered together on the main street, talking and watching the store.

It would be untrue to say that all the town took part in this evil festival. There were a few sensible men who reasoned that Miss Amelia, being rich, would not go out of her way to murder a vagabond for a few trifles of junk. In the town there were even three good people, and they did not want this crime, not even for the sake of the interest and the great commotion it would entail; it gave them no pleasure to think of Miss Amelia holding to the bars of the penitentiary and being electrocuted in Atlanta. These good people judged Miss Amelia in a different way from what the others judged her. When a person is as contrary in every single respect as she was and when the sins of a person have amounted to such a point that they can hardly be remembered all at once —then this person plainly requires a special judgment. They remembered that Miss Amelia had been born dark and somewhat queer of face, raised motherless by her father who was a solitary man, that early in youth she had grown to be six feet two inches tall which in itself is not natural for a woman, and that her ways and habits of life were too peculiar ever to reason about. Above all, they remembered her puzzling marriage, which was the most unreasonable scandal ever to happen in this town.

So these good people felt toward her something near to pity. And when she was out on her wild business, such as rushing in a house to drag forth a sewing machine in payment for a debt, or getting herself worked up over some matter concerning the law—they had toward her a feeling which was a mixture of exasperation, a ridiculous little inside tickle, and a deep, unnamable sadness. But enough of the good people, for there were only three of them; the rest of the town was making a holiday of this fancied crime the whole of the afternoon.

Miss Amelia herself, for some strange reason, seemed unaware of all this. She spent most of her day upstairs. When down in the store, she prowled around peacefully, her hands deep in the pockets of her overalls and head bent so low that her chin was tucked inside the collar of her shirt. There was no bloodstain on her anywhere. Often she stopped and just stood somberly looking down at the cracks in the floor, twisting a lock of her short-cropped hair, and whispering something to herself. But most of the day was spent upstairs.

Dark came on. The rain that afternoon had chilled the air, so that the evening was bleak and gloomy as in wintertime. There were no stars in the sky, and a light, icy drizzle had set in. The lamps in the houses made mournful, wavering flickers when watched from the street. A wind had come up, not from the swamp side of the town but from the cold black pinewoods to the north.

The clocks in the town struck eight. Still nothing had happened. The bleak night, after the gruesome talk of the day, put a fear in some people, and they stayed home close to the fire. Others were gathered in groups together. Some eight or ten men had convened on the porch of Miss Amelia's store. They were silent and were indeed just waiting about. They themselves did not know what they were waiting for, but it was this: in times of tension, when some great action is impending, men gather and wait in this way. And after a time there will come a moment when all together they will act in unison, not from thought or from the will of any one

15

man, but as though their instincts had merged together so that the decision belongs to no single one of them, but to the group as a whole. At such a time, no individual hesitates. And whether the matter will be settled peaceably, or whether the joint action will result in ransacking, violence, and crime, depends on destiny. So the men waited soberly on the porch of Miss Amelia's store, not one of them realizing what they would do, but knowing inwardly that they must wait, and that the time had almost come.

Now the door to the store was open. Inside it was bright and natural-looking. To the left was the counter where slabs of white meat, rock candy, and tobacco were kept. Behind this were shelves of salted white meat and meal. The right side of the store was mostly filled with farm implements and such. At the back of the store, to the left, was the door leading up the stairs, and it was open. And at the far right of the store there was another door which led to a little room that Miss Amelia called her office. This door was also open. And at eight o'clock that evening Miss Amelia could be seen there sitting before her rolltop desk, figuring with a fountain pen and some pieces of paper.

The office was cheerfully lighted, and Miss Amelia did not seem to notice the delegation on the porch. Everything around her was in great order, as usual. This office was a room well-known, in a dreadful way, throughout the country. It was there Miss Amelia transacted all business. On the desk was a carefully covered typewriter which she knew how to run, but used only for the most important documents. In the drawers were literally thousands of papers, all filed according to the alphabet. This office was also the place where Miss Amelia received sick people, for she enjoyed doctoring and did a great deal of it. Two whole shelves were crowded with bottles and various paraphernalia. Against the wall was a bench where the patients sat. She could sew up a wound with a burnt needle so that it would not turn green. For burns she had a cool, sweet syrup. For unlocated sickness there were any number of different medicines which she had brewed herself from unknown recipes. They wrenched loose the bowels very well, but they could not be given to small children, as they caused bad convulsions; for them she had an entirely separate draught, gentler and sweet-flavored. Yes, all in all, she was considered a good doctor. Her hands, though very large and bony, had a light touch about them. She possessed great imagination and used hundreds of different cures. In the face of the most dangerous and extraordinary treatment she did not hesitate, and no disease was so terrible but what she would undertake to cure it. In this there was one exception. If a patient came with a female complaint she could do nothing. Indeed at the mere mention of the words her face would slowly darken with shame, and she would stand there craning her neck against the collar of her shirt, or rubbing her swamp boots together, for all the world like a great, shamed, dumb-tongued child. But in other matters people trusted her. She charged no fees whatsoever and always had a raft of patients.

On this evening, Miss Amelia wrote with her fountain pen a good deal. But even so she could not be forever unaware of the group waiting out there on the dark porch, and watching her. From time to time she looked up and regarded them steadily. But she did not holler out to them to demand why they were loafing around her property like a sorry bunch of gabbies. Her face was proud and stern, as it always was when she sat at the desk of her office. After a time their peering in like that seemed to annoy her. She wiped her cheek with a red handkerchief, got up, and closed the office door.

Now to the group on the porch this gesture acted as a signal. The time had come. They had stood for a long while with the night raw and gloomy in the street behind them. They had waited long and just at that moment the instinct to act came on them. All at once, as though moved by one will, they walked into the store. At that moment the eight men looked very much alike

—all wearing blue overalls, most of them with whitish hair, all pale of face, and all with a set, dreaming look in the eye. What they would have done next no one knows. But at that instant there was a noise at the head of the staircase. The men looked up and then stood dumb with shock. It was the hunchback, whom they had already murdered in their minds. Also, the creature was not at all as had been pictured to them—not a pitiful and dirty little chatterer, alone and beggared in this world. Indeed, he was like nothing any man among them had ever beheld until that time. The room was still as death.

The hunchback came down slowly with the proudness of one who owns every plank of the floor beneath his feet. In the past days he had greatly changed. For one thing he was clean beyond words. He still wore his little coat, but it was brushed off and neatly mended. Beneath this was a fresh red and black checkered shirt belonging to Miss Amelia. He did not wear trousers such as ordinary men are meant to wear, but a pair of tight-fitting little knee-length breeches. On his skinny legs he wore black stockings, and his shoes were of a special kind, being queerly shaped, laced up over the ankles, and newly cleaned and polished with wax. Around his neck, so that his large, pale ears were almost completely covered, he wore a shawl of lime-green wool, the fringes of which almost touched the floor.

The hunchback walked down the store with his stiff little strut and then stood in the center of the group that had come inside. They cleared a space about him and stood looking with hands loose at their sides and eyes wide open. The hunchback himself got his bearings in an odd manner. He regarded each person steadily at his own eye-level, which was about belt line for an ordinary man. Then with shrewd deliberation he examined each man's lower regions—from the waist to the sole of the shoe. When he had satisfied himself he closed his eyes for a moment and shook his head, as though in his opinion what he had seen did not amount to much.

Then with assurance, only to confirm himself, he tilted back his head and took in the halo of faces around him with one long, circling stare. There was a half-filled sack of guano on the left side of the store, and when he had found his bearings in this way, the hunchback sat down upon it. Cozily settled, with his little legs crossed, he took from his coat pocket a certain object.

Now it took some moments for the men in the store to regain their ease. Merlie Ryan, he of the three-day fever who had started the rumor that day, was the first to speak. He looked at the object which the hunchback was fondling, and said in a hushed voice:

'What is it you have there?'

Each man knew well what it was the hunchback was handling. For it was the snuffbox which had belonged to Miss Amelia's father. The snuffbox was of blue enamel with a dainty embellishment of wrought gold on the lid. The group knew it well and marveled. They glanced warily at the closed office door, and heard the low sound of Miss Amelia whistling to herself.

'Yes, what is it, Peanut?'

The hunchback looked up quickly and sharpened his mouth to speak. 'Why, this is a lay-low to catch meddlers.'

The hunchback reached in the box with his scrambly little fingers and ate something, but he offered no one around him a taste. It was not even proper snuff which he was taking, but a mixture of sugar and cocoa. This he took, though, as snuff, pocketing a little wad of it beneath his lower lip and licking down neatly into this with a flick of his tongue which made a frequent grimace come over his face.

'The very teeth in my head have always tasted sour to me,' he said in explanation. 'That is the reason why I take this kind of sweet snuff.'

The group still clustered around, feeling somewhat gawky and bewildered. This sensation never quite wore off, but it was soon tempered by another feeling—an air of intimacy in the room and a vague festivity. Now the

19

names of the men of the group there on that evening were as follows: Hasty Malone, Robert Calvert Hale, Merlie Ryan, Reverend T. M. Willin, Rosser Cline, Rip Wellborn, Henry Ford Crimp, and Horace Wells. Except for Reverend Willin, they are all alike in many ways as has been said—all having taken pleasure from something or other, all having wept and suffered in some way, most of them tractable unless exasperated. Each of them worked in the mill, and lived with others in a two- or three-room house for which the rent was ten dollars or twelve dollars a month. All had been paid that afternoon, for it was Saturday. So, for the present, think of them as a whole.

The hunchback, however, was already sorting them out in his mind. Once comfortably settled he began to chat with everyone, asking questions such as if a man was married, how old he was, how much his wages came to in an average week, et cetera—picking his way along to inquiries which were downright intimate. Soon the group was joined by others in the town, Henry Macy, idlers who had sensed something extraordinary, women come to fetch their men who lingered on, and even one loose, towhead child who tiptoed into the store, stole a box of animal crackers, and made off very quietly. So the premises of Miss Amelia were soon crowded, and she herself had not yet opened her office door.

There is a type of person who has a quality about him that sets him apart from other and more ordinary human beings. Such a person has an instinct which is usually found only in small children, an instinct to establish immediate and vital contact between himself and all things in the world. Certainly the hunchback was of this type. He had only been in the store half an hour before an immediate contact had been established between him and each other individual. It was as though he had lived in the town for years, was a well-known character, and had been sitting and talking there on that guano sack for countless evenings. This, together with the fact that it was Saturday night, could account for the air of freedom and illicit gladness in the store. There was a tension, also, partly because of the oddity of the situation and because Miss Amelia was still closed off in her office and had not yet made her appearance.

She came out that evening at ten o'clock. And those who were expecting some drama at her entrance were disappointed. She opened the door and walked in with her slow, gangling swagger. There was a streak of ink on one side of her nose, and she had knotted the red handkerchief about her neck. She seemed to notice nothing unusual. Her gray, crossed eyes glanced over to the place where the hunchback was sitting, and for a moment lingered there. The rest of the crowd in her store she regarded with only a peaceable surprise.

'Does anyone want waiting on?' she asked quietly.

There were a number of customers, because it was Saturday night, and they all wanted liquor. Now Miss Amelia had dug up an aged barrel only three days past and had siphoned it into bottles back by the still. This night she took the money from the customers and counted it beneath the bright light. Such was the ordinary procedure. But after this what happened was not ordinary. Always before, it was necessary to go around to the dark back yard, and there she would hand out your bottle through the kitchen door. There was no feeling of joy in the transaction. After getting his liquor the customer walked off into the night. Or, if his wife would not have it in the home, he was allowed to come back around to the front porch of the store and guzzle there or in the street. Now, both the porch and the street before it were the property of Miss Amelia, and no mistake about it—but she did not regard them as her premises; the premises began at the front door and took in the entire inside of the building. There she had never allowed liquor to be opened or drunk by anyone but herself. Now for the first time she broke this rule. She went to the kitchen, with the hunchback close at her heels, and she brought back the bottles into the warm, bright store. More than that she furnished some glasses and opened two boxes of crackers so that they were there hospitably in a platter on the counter and anyone who wished could take one free.

She spoke to no one but the hunchback, and she only asked him in a somewhat harsh and husky voice: "Cousin Lymon, will you have yours straight, or warmed in a pan with water on the stove?"

'If you please, Amelia,' the hunchback said. (And since what time had anyone presumed to address Miss Amelia by her bare name, without a title of respect?— Certainly not her bridegroom and her husband of ten days. In fact, not since the death of her father, who for some reason had always called her Little, had anyone dared to address her in such a familiar way.) 'If you please, I'll have it warmed.'

Now, this was the beginning of the café. It was as simple as that. Recall that the night was gloomy as in wintertime, and to have sat around the property outside would have made a sorry celebration. But inside there was company and a genial warmth. Someone had rattled up the stove in the rear, and those who bought bottles shared their liquor with friends. Several women were there and they had twists of licorice, a Nehi, or even a swallow of the whisky. The hunchback was still a novelty and his presence amused everyone. The bench in the office was brought in, together with several extra chairs. Other people leaned against the counter or made themselves comfortable on barrels and sacks. Nor did the opening of liquor on the premises cause any rambunctiousness, indecent giggles, or misbehavior whatsoever. On the contrary the company was polite even to the point of a certain timidity. For people in this town were then unused to gathering together for the sake of pleasure. They met to work in the mill. Or on Sunday there would be an all-day camp meeting—and though that is a pleasure, the intention of the whole affair is to sharpen your view of Hell and put into you a keen fear of the Lord Almighty. But the spirit of a café is altogether different. Even the richest, greediest old rascal will behave himself, insulting no one in a proper café. And poor people look about them gratefully and pinch up the salt in a dainty and modest manner. For the atmosphere of a proper café implies these qualities: fellowship, the satisfactions of the belly, and a certain gaiety and grace of behavior. This had never been told to the gathering in Miss Amelia's store that night. But they knew it of themselves, although never, of course, until that time had there been a café in the town.

Now, the cause of all this, Miss Amelia, stood most of the evening in the doorway leading to the kitchen. Outwardly she did not seem changed at all. But there were many who noticed her face. She watched all that went on, but most of the time her eyes were fastened lonesomely on the hunchback. He strutted about the store, eating from his snuffbox, and being at once sour and agreeable. Where Miss Amelia stood, the light from the chinks of the stove cast a glow, so that her brown, long face was somewhat brightened. She seemed to be looking inward. There was in her expression pain, perplexity, and uncertain joy. Her lips were not so firmly set as usual, and she swallowed often. Her skin had paled and her large empty hands were sweating. Her look that night, then, was the lonesome look of the lover.

This opening of the café came to an end at midnight. Everyone said good-bye to everyone else in a friendly fashion. Miss Amelia shut the front door of her premises, but forgot to bolt it. Soon everything—the main street with its three stores, the mill, the houses—all the town, in fact—was dark and silent. And so ended three days and nights in which had come an arrival of a stranger, an unholy holiday, and the start of the café.

Now time must pass. For the next four years are much alike. There are great changes, but these changes are brought about bit by bit, in simple steps which in themselves do not appear to be important. The hunchback continued to live with Miss Amelia. The café expanded in a gradual way. Miss Amelia began to sell her liquor by the drink, and some tables were brought into the store. There were customers every evening, and on Saturday a great crowd. Miss Amelia began to serve fried catfish suppers at fifteen cents a plate. The hunchback cajoled her into buying a fine mechanical piano. Within two years the place was a store no longer, but had been converted into a proper café, open every evening from six until twelve o'clock.

Each night the hunchback came down the stairs with the air of one who has a grand opinion of himself. He always smelled slightly of turnip greens, as Miss Amelia rubbed him night and morning with pot liquor to give him strength. She spoiled him to a point beyond reason, but nothing seemed to strengthen him; food only made his hump and his head grow larger while the rest of him remained weakly and deformed. Miss Amelia was the same in appearance. During the week she still wore swamp boots and overalls, but on Sunday she put on a dark red dress that hung on her in a most peculiar fashion. Her manners, however, and her way of life were greatly changed. She still loved a fierce lawsuit, but she was not so quick to cheat her fellow man and to exact cruel payments. Because the hunchback was so extremely sociable, she even went about a little—to revivals, to funerals, and so forth. Her doctoring was as successful as ever, her liquor even finer than before, if that were possible. The café itself proved profitable and was the only place of pleasure for many miles around.

So for the moment regard these years from random and disjointed views. See the hunchback marching in Miss Amelia's footsteps when on a red winter morning they set out for the pinewoods to hunt. See them working on her properties—with Cousin Lymon standing by and doing absolutely nothing, but quick to point out any laziness among the hands. On autumn afternoons they sat on the back steps chopping sugar cane. The glaring summer days they spent back in the swamp where the water cypress is a deep black green, where beneath the tangled swamp trees there is a drowsy gloom. When the path leads through a bog or a stretch of blackened water see Miss Amelia bend down to let Cousin Lymon scramble on her back—and see her wading forward with the hunchback settled on her shoulders, clinging to her ears or to her broad forehead. Occasionally Miss Amelia cranked up the Ford which she had bought and treated Cousin Lymon to a picture-show in Cheehaw, or to some distant fair or cockfight; the hunchback took a passionate delight in spectacles. Of course, they were in their café every morning, they would often sit for hours together by the fireplace in the parlor upstairs. For the hunchback was sickly at night and dreaded to lie looking into the dark. He had a deep fear of death. And Miss Amelia would not leave him by himself to suffer with this fright. It may even be reasoned that the growth of the café came about mainly on this account; it was a thing that brought him company and pleasure and that helped him through the night. So compose from such flashes an image of these years as a whole. And for a moment let it rest.

Now some explanation is due for all this behavior. The time has come to speak about love. For Miss Amelia loved Cousin Lymon. So much was clear to everyone. They lived in the same house together and were never seen apart. Therefore, according to Mrs. MacPhail, a warty-nosed old busybody who is continually moving her sticks of furniture from one part of the front room to another; according to her and to certain others, these two were living in sin. If they were related, they were only a cross between first and second cousins, and even that could in no way be proved. Now, of course, Miss Amelia was a powerful blunderbuss of a person, more than six feet tall—and Cousin Lymon a weakly little hunchback reaching only to her waist. But so much the better for Mrs. Stumpy MacPhail and her cronies, for they and their kind glory in conjunctions which are ill-matched and pitiful. So let them be. The good people thought that if those two had found some satisfaction of the flesh between themselves, then it was a matter concerning them and God alone. All sensible people agreed in their opinion about this conjecture—and their answer was a plain, flat top. What sort of thing, then, was this love?

First of all, love is a joint experience between two persons—but the fact that it is a joint experience does not mean that it is a similar experience to the two people involved. There are the lover and the beloved, but these two come from different countries. Often the beloved is only a stimulus for all the stored-up love which has lain quiet within the lover for a long time hitherto. And somehow every lover knows this. He feels in his soul that his love is a solitary thing. He comes to know a new, strange loneliness and it is this knowledge which makes him suffer. So there is only one thing for the lover to do. He must house his love within himself as best he can; he must create for himself a whole new inward world—a world intense and strange, complete in himself. Let it be added here that this lover about whom we speak need not necessarily be a young man saving for a wedding ring—this lover can be man, woman, child, or indeed any human creature on this earth.

Now, the beloved can also be of any description. The most outlandish people can be the stimulus for love. A man may be a doddering great-grandfather and still love only a strange girl he saw in the streets of Cheehaw one afternoon two decades past. The preacher may love a fallen woman. The beloved may be treacherous, greasy-headed, and given to evil habits. Yes, and the lover may see this as clearly as anyone else—but that does not affect the evolution of his love one whit. A most mediocre person can be the object of a love which is wild, extravagant, and beautiful as the poison lilies of the swamp. A good man may be the stimulus for a love both violent and debased, or a jabbering madman may bring about in the soul of someone a tender and simple idyll. Therefore, the value and quality of any love is determined solely by the lover himself.

It is for this reason that most of us would rather love than be loved. Almost everyone wants to be the lover. And the curt truth is that, in a deep secret way, the state of being be loved is intolerable to many. The beloved fears and hates the lover, and with the best of reasons. For the lover is forever trying to strip bare his beloved. The lover craves any possible relation with the beloved, even if this experience can cause him only pain.

It has been mentioned before that Miss Amelia was once married. And this curious episode might as well be accounted for at this point. Remember that it all happened long ago, and that it was Miss Amelia's only personal contact, before the hunchback came to her, with this phenomenon—love.

The town then was the same as it is now, except there were two stores instead of three and the peach trees along the street were more crooked and smaller than they are now. Miss Amelia was nineteen years old at the time, and her father had been dead many months. There was in the town at that time a loom-fixer named Marvin Macy. He was the brother of Henry Macy, although to know them you would never guess that those two could be kin. For Marvin Macy was the handsomest man in this region—being six feet one inch tall, hard-muscled, and with slow gray eyes and curly hair. He was well off, made good wages, and had a gold watch which opened in the back to a picture of a waterfall. From the outward and worldly point of view Marvin Macy was a fortunate fellow; he needed to bow and scrape to no one and always got just what he wanted. But from a more serious and thoughtful viewpoint Marvin Macy was not a person to be envied, for he was an evil character. His reputation was as bad, if not worse, than that of any young man in the county. For years, when he was a boy, he had carried about with him the dried and salted ear of a man he had killed in a razor fight. He had chopped off the tails of squirrels in the pinewoods just to please his fancy, and in his left hip picket he carried forbidden marijuana weed to tempt those who were discouraged and drawn toward death. Yet in spite of his well-known reputation he was the beloved of many females in this region—and there were at the time several young girls who were clean-haired and soft-eyed, with tender sweet little buttocks and charming ways. These gentle young girls he degraded and shamed. Then finally, at the age of twenty-two, this Marvin Macy chose Miss Amelia. That solitary, gangling, queer-eyed girl was the one he longed for. Nor did he want her because of her money, but solely out of love.

And love changed Marvin Macy. Before the time when he loved Miss Amelia it could be questioned if such a person had within him a heart and soul. Yet there is some explanation for the ugliness of his character, for Marvin Macy had had a hard beginning in this world. He was one of seven unwanted children whose parents could hardly be called parents at all; these parents were wild younguns who liked to fish and roam around the swamp. Their own children, and there was a new one almost every year, were only a nuisance to them. At night when they came home from the mill they would look at the children as though they did not know wherever they had come from. If the children cried they were beaten, and the first thing they learned in this world was to seek the darkest corner of the room and try to hide themselves as best they could. They were as thin as little whitehaired ghosts, and they did not speak, not even to each other. Finally, they were abandoned by their parents altogether and left to the mercies of the town. It was a hard winter, with the mill closed down almost three months, and much misery everywhere. But this is not a town to let white orphans perish in the road before your eyes. So here is what came about: the eldest child, who was eight years old, walked into Cheehaw and disappeared—perhaps he took a freight train somewhere and went out into the world, nobody knows. Three other children were boarded out amongst the town, being sent around from one kitchen to another, and as they were delicate they died before Easter time. The last two children were Marvin Macy and Henry Macy, and they were taken into a home. There was a good woman in the town named Mrs. Mary Hale, and she took Marvin Macy and Henry Macy and loved them as her own. They were raised in her household and treated well.

But the hearts of small children are delicate organs. A cruel beginning in this world can twist them into curious shapes. The heart of a hurt child can shrink so that forever afterward it is hard and pitted as the seed of a peach. Or again, the heart of such a child may fester and swell until it is a misery to carry within the body, easily chafed and hurt by the most ordinary things. This last is what happened to Henry Macy, who is so opposite to his brother, is the kindest and gentlest man in town. He lends his wages to those who are unfortunate, and in the old days he used to care for the children whose parents were at the café on Saturday night. But he is a shy man, and he has the look of one who has a swollen heart and suffers. Marvin Macy, however, grew to be bold and fearless and cruel. His heart turned tough as the horns of Satan, and until the time when he loved Miss Amelia he brought to his brother and the good woman who raised him nothing but shame and trouble.

But love reversed the character of Marvin Macy. For two years he loved Miss Amelia, but he did not declare himself. He would stand near the door of her premises, his cap in his hand, his eyes meek and longing and misty gray. He reformed himself completely. He was good to his brother and foster mother, and he saved his wages and learned thrift. Moreover, he reached out toward God. No longer did he lie around on the floor of the front porch all day Sunday, singing and playing his guitar; he attended church services and was present at all religious meetings. He learned good manners: he trained himself to rise and give his chair to a lady, and he quit swearing and fighting and using holy names in vain. So for two years he passed through this transformation and improved his character in every way. Then at the end of the two years he went one evening to Miss Amelia, carrying a bunch of swamp flowers, a sack of chitterlins, and a silver ring—that night Marvin Macy declared himself.

And Miss Amelia married him. Later everyone wondered why. Some said it was because she wanted to get herself some wedding presents. Others believed it came about through the nagging of Miss Amelia's great-aunt in Cheehaw, who was a terrible old woman. Anyway, she strode with great steps down the aisle of the church wearing her dead mother's bridal gown, which was of yellow satin and at least twelve inches too short for her. It was a winter afternoon and the clear sun shone through the ruby windows of the church and put a curious glow on the pair before the altar. As the marriage lines were read Miss Amelia kept making an odd gesture —she would rub the palm of her right hand down the side of her satin wedding gown. She was reaching for the pocket of her overalls, and being unable to find it her face became impatient, bored, and exasperated. At last when the lines were spoken and the marriage prayer was done Miss Amelia hurried out of the church, not taking the arm of her husband, but walking at least two paces ahead of him.

The church is no distance from the store so the bride and groom walked home. It is said that on the way Miss Amelia began to talk about some deal she had worked up with a farmer over a load of kindling wood. In fact, she treated her groom in exactly the same manner she would have used with some customer who had come into the store to buy a pint from her. But so far all had gone decently enough; the town was gratified, as people had seen what this love had done to Marvin Macy and hoped that it might also reform his bride. At least, they counted on the marriage to tone down

Miss Amelia's temper, to put a bit of bride-fat on her, and to change her at last into a calculable woman.

They were wrong. The young boys who watched through the window on that night said that this is what actually happened: The bride and groom ate a grand supper prepared by Jeff, the old Negro who cooked for Miss Amelia. The bride took second servings of everything, but the groom picked with his food. Then the bride went about her ordinary business—reading the newspaper, finishing an inventory of the stock in the store, and so forth. The groom hung about in the doorway with a loose, foolish, blissful face and was not noticed. At eleven o'clock the bride took a lamp and went upstairs. The groom followed close behind her. So far all had gone decently enough, but what followed after was unholy.

Within half an hour Miss Amelia had stomped down the stairs in breeches and a khaki jacket. Her face had darkened so that it looked quite black. She slammed the kitchen door and gave it an ugly kick. Then she controlled herself. She poked up the fire, sat down, and put her feet up on the kitchen stove. She read the Farmer's Almanac, drank coffee, and had a smoke with her father's pipe. Her face was hard, stern, and had now whitened to its natural color. Sometimes she paused to jot down some information from the Almanac on a piece of paper. Toward dawn she went into her office and uncovered her typewriter, which she had recently bought and was only just learning how to run. That was the way in which she spent the whole of her wedding night. At daylight she went out to her yard as though nothing whatsoever had occurred and did some carpentering on a rabbit hutch which she had begun the week before and intended to sell somewhere.

A groom is in a sorry fix when he is unable to bring his well-beloved bride to bed with him, and the whole town knows it. Marvin Macy came down that day still in his wedding finery, and with a sick face. God knows how he had spent the night. He moped about the yard,

31

watching Miss Amelia, but keeping some distance away from her. Then toward noon an idea came to him and he went off in the direction of Society City. He returned with presents—an opal ring, a pink enamel doreen of the sort which was then in fashion, a silver bracelet with two hearts on it, and a box of candy which had cost two dollars and a half. Miss Amelia looked over these fine gifts and opened the box of candy, for she was hungry. The rest of the presents she judged shrewdly for a moment to sum up their value—then she put them in the counter out for sale. The night was spent in much the same manner as the preceding one—except that Miss Amelia brought her feather mattress to make a pallet by the kitchen stove, and she slept fairly well.

Things went on like this for three days. Miss Amelia went about her business as usual, and took great interest in some rumor that a bridge was to be built some ten miles down the road. Marvin Macy still followed her about around the premises, and it was plain from his face how he suffered. Then on the fourth day he did an extremely simple-minded thing: he went to Cheehaw and came back with a lawyer. Then in Miss Amelia's office he signed over to her the whole of his worldly goods, which was ten acres of timberland which he had bought with the money he had saved. She studied the paper sternly to make sure there was no possibility of a trick and filed it soberly in the drawer of her desk. That afternoon Marvin Macy took a quart bottle of whisky and went with it alone out in the swamp while the sun was still shining. Toward evening he came in drunk, went up to Miss Amelia with wet wide eyes, and put his hand on her shoulder. He was trying to tell her something, but before he could open his mouth she had swung once with her fist and hit his face so hard that he was thrown back against the wall and one of his front teeth was broken.

The rest of this affair can only be mentioned in bare outline. After this first blow Miss Amelia hit him whenever he came within arm's reach of her, and whenever he was drunk. At last she turned him off the premises altogether, and he was forced to suffer publicly. During the day he hung around just outside the boundary line of Miss Amelia's property and sometimes with a drawn crazy look he would fetch his rifle and sit there cleaning it, peering at Miss Amelia steadily. If she was afraid she did not show it, but her face was sterner than ever, and often she spat on the ground. His last foolish effort was to climb in the window of her store one night and to sit there in the dark, for no purpose whatsoever, until she came down the stairs next morning. For this Miss Amelia set off immediately to the courthouse in Cheehaw with some notion that she could get him locked in the penitentiary for trespassing. Marvin Macy left the town that day, and no one saw him go, or knew just where he went. On leaving he put a long curious letter, partly written in pencil and partly with ink, beneath Miss Amelia's door. It was a wild love letter— but in it were also included threats, and he swore that in his life he would get even with her. His marriage had lasted for ten days. And the town felt the special satisfaction that people feel when someone has been thoroughly done in by some scandalous and terrible means.

Miss Amelia was left with everything that Marvin Macy had ever owned—his timberwood, his gilt watch, every one of his possessions. But she seemed to attach little value to them and that spring she cut up his Klansman's robe to cover her tobacco plants. So all that he had ever done was to make her richer and to bring her love. But, strange to say, she never spoke of him but with a terrible and spiteful bitterness. She never once referred to him by name but always mentioned him scornfully as 'that loom-fixer I was married to.'

And later, when horrifying rumors concerning Marvin Macy reached the town, Miss Amelia was very pleased. For the true character of Marvin Macy finally revealed itself, once he had freed himself of his love. He became a criminal whose picture and whose name were in all the papers in the state. He robbed three filling stations and held up the A & P store of Society City with a sawed-off gun. He was suspected of the murder of Slit-Eye Sam who was a noted highjacker. All these crimes were connected with the name of Marvin Macy, so that his evil became famous through many countries. Then finally the law captured him, drunk, on the floor of a tourist cabin, his guitar by his side, and fifty-seven dollars in his right shoe. He was tried, sentenced, and sent off to the penitentiary near Atlanta. Miss Amelia was deeply gratified.

Well, all this happened a long time ago, and it is the story of Miss Amelia's marriage. The town laughed a long time over this grotesque affair. But though the outward facts of this love are indeed sad and ridiculous, it must be remembered that the real story was that which took place in the soul of the lover himself. So who but God can be the final judge of this or any other love? On the very first night of the café there were several who suddenly thought of this broken bridegroom, locked in the gloomy penitentiary, many miles away. And in the years that followed, Marvin Macy was not altogether forgotten in the town. His name was never mentioned in the presence of Miss Amelia or the hunchback. But the memory of his passion and his crimes, and the thought of him trapped in his cell in the penitentiary, was like a troubling undertone beneath the happy love of Miss Amelia and the gaiety of the café. So do not forget this Marvin Macy, as he is to act a terrible part in the story which is yet to come.

During the four years in which the store became a café the rooms upstairs were not changed. This part of the premises remained exactly as it had been all of Miss Amelia's life, as it was in the time of her father, and most likely his father before him. The three rooms, it is already known, were immaculately clean. The smallest object had its exact place, and everything was wiped and dusted by Jeff, the servant of Miss Amelia, each morning. The front room belonged to Cousin Lymon—it was the room where Marvin Macy had stayed during the few nights he was allowed on the premises, and before that it was the bedroom of Miss Amelia's father. The room was furnished with a large chifforobe, a bureau covered with a stiff white linen cloth crocheted at the edges, and a marble-topped table. The bed was immense, an old fourposter made of carved, dark rosewood. On it were two feather mattresses, bolsters, and a number of handmade comforts. The bed was so high that beneath it were two wooden steps—no occupant had ever used these steps before, but Cousin Lymon drew them out each night and walked up in state. Beside the steps, but pushed modestly out of view, there was a china chamber-pot painted with pink roses. No rug covered the dark, polished floor and the curtains were of some white stuff, also crocheted at the edges.

On the other side of the parlor was Miss Amelia's bedroom, and it was smaller and very simple. The bed was narrow and made of pine. There was a bureau for her breeches, shirts, and Sunday dress, and she had hammered two nails in the closet wall on which to hang her swamp boots. There were no curtains, rugs, or ornaments of any kind.

The large middle room, the parlor, was elaborate. The rosewood sofa, upholstered in threadbare green silk, was before the fireplace. Marble-topped tables, two Singer sewing machines, a big vase of pampas grass—everything was rich and grand. The most important piece of furniture in the parlor was a big, glassed-doored cabinet in which was kept a number of treasures and curios. Miss Amelia had added two objects to this collection—one was a large acorn from a water oak, the other a little velvet box holding two small, grayish stones. Sometimes when she had nothing much to do, Miss Amelia would take out this velvet box and stand by the window with the stones in the palm of her hand, looking down at them with a mixture of fascination, dubious respect, and fear. They were the kidney stones of Miss Amelia herself, and had been taken from her by the doctor in Cheehaw some years ago. It had been a terrible experience, from the first minute to the last, and all she had got out of it were those two little stones; she was bound to set great store by them, or else admit to a mighty sorry bargain. So she kept them and in the second year of Cousin Lymon's stay with her she had them set as ornaments in a watch chain which she gave to him. The other object she had added to the collection, the large acorn, was precious to her—but when she looked at it her face was always saddened and perplexed.

'Amelia, what does it signify?' Cousin Lymon asked her.

'Why, it's just an acorn,' she answered. 'Just an acorn I picked up on the afternoon Big Papa died.'

'How do you mean?' Cousin Lymon insisted.

'I mean it's just an acorn I spied on the ground that day. I picked it up and put it in my pocket. But I don't know why.'

'What a peculiar reason to keep it,' Cousin Lymon said.

The talks of Miss Amelia and Cousin Lymon in the rooms upstairs, usually in the first few hours of the morning when the hunchback could not sleep, were many. As a rule, Miss Amelia was a silent woman, not letting her tongue run wild on any subject that happened to pop into her head. There were certain topics of conversation, however, in which she took pleasure. All these subjects had one point in common—they were interminable. She liked to contemplate problems which could be worked over for decades and still remain insoluble. Cousin Lymon, on the other hand, enjoyed talking on any subject whatsoever, as he was a great chatterer. Their approach to any conversation was altogether different. Miss Amelia always kept to the broad, rambling generalities of the matter, going on endlessly in a low, thoughtful voice and getting nowhere —while Cousin Lymon would interrupt her suddenly to pick up, magpie fashion, some detail which, even if unimportant, was at least concrete and bearing on some practical facet close at hand. Some of the favorite subjects of Miss Amelia were: the stars, the reason why Negroes are black, the best treatment for cancer, and so forth. Her father was also an interminable subject which was dear to her.

'Why, Law,' she would say to Lymon. 'Those days I slept. I'd go to bed just as the lamp was turned on and sleep—why, I'd sleep like I was drowned in warm axle grease. Then come daybreak Big Papa would walk in and put his hand down on my shoulder. "Get stirring, Little," he would say. Then later he would holler up the stairs from the kitchen when the stove was hot. "Fried grits," he would holler. "White meat and gravy. Ham and eggs." And I'd run down the stairs and dress by the hot stove while he was out washing at the pump. Then off we'd go to the still or maybe——'

'The grits we had this morning was poor,' Cousin Lymon said. 'Fried too quick so that the inside never heated.'

'And when Big Papa would run off the liquor in those days——' The conversation would go on endlessly, with Miss Amelia's long legs stretched out before the hearth; for winter or summer there was always a fire in the grate, as Lymon was cold-natured. He sat in a low chair across from her, his feet not quite touching the floor and his torso usually well-wrapped in a blanket or the green wool shawl. Miss Amelia never mentioned her father to anyone else except Cousin Lymon.

That was one of the ways in which she showed her love for him. He had her confidence in the most delicate and vital matters. He alone knew where she kept the chart that showed where certain barrels of whisky were buried on a piece of property near by. He alone had access to her bank-book and the key to the cabinet of curios. He took money from the cash register, whole handfuls of it, and appreciated the loud jingle it made inside his pockets. He owned almost everything on the premises, for when he was cross Miss Amelia would prowl about and find him some present—so that now there was hardly anything left close at hand to give him. The only part of her life that she did not want Cousin Lymon to share with her was the memory of her ten-day marriage. Marvin Macy was the one subject that was never, at any time, discussed between the two of them.

So let the slow years pass and come to a Saturday evening six years after the time when Cousin Lymon came first to the town. It was August and the sky had burned above the town like a sheet of flame all day. Now the green twilight was near and there was a feeling of repose. The street was coated an inch deep with dry golden dust and the little children ran about half-naked, sneezed often, sweated, and were fretful. The mill had closed down at noon. People in the houses along the main street sat resting on their steps and the women had palmetto fans. At Miss Amelia's there was a sign at the front of the premises saying CAFE. The back porch was cool with latticed shadows and there cousin Lymon sat turning the ice-cream freezer—often he unpacked the salt and ice and removed the dasher to lick a bit and see how the work was coming on. Jeff cooked in the kitchen. Early that morning Miss Amelia had put a notice on the wall of the front porch reading: Chicken Dinner—Twenty Cents Tonite. The café was already open and Miss Amelia had just finished a period of work in her office. All the eight tables were occupied and from the mechanical piano came a jingling tune.

In a corner near the door and sitting at a table with a child, was Henry Macy. He was drinking a glass of liquor, which was unusual for him, as liquor went easily to his head and made him cry or sing. His face was very pale and his left eye worked constantly in a nervous tic, as it was apt to do when he was agitated. He had come into the café sidewise and silent, and when he was greeted he did not speak. The child next to him belonged to Horace Wells, and he had been left at Miss Amelia's that morning to be doctored.

Miss Amelia came out from her office in good spirits. She attended to a few details in the kitchen and entered the café with the pope's nose of a hen between her fingers, as that was her favorite piece. She looked about the room, saw that in general all was well, and went over to the corner table by Henry Macy. She turned the chair around and sat straddling the back, as she only wanted to pass the time of day and was not yet ready for her supper. There was a bottle of Kroup Kure in the hip pocket of her overalls—a medicine made from whisky, rock candy, and a secret ingredient. Miss Amelia uncorked the bottle and put it to the mouth of the child. Then she turned to Henry Macy and, seeing the nervous winking of his left eye, she asked:

'What ails you?'

Henry Macy seemed on the point of saying something difficult, but, after a long look into the eyes of Miss Amelia, he swallowed and did not speak.

So Miss Amelia returned to her patient. Only the child's head showed above the table top. His face was very red, with the eyelids half-closed and the mouth partly open. He had a large, hard, swollen boil on his thigh, and had been brought to Miss Amelia so that it could be opened. But Miss Amelia used a special method with children; she did not like to see them hurt, struggling, and terrified. So she had kept the child around the premises all day, giving him licorice and frequent doses of the Kroup Kure, and toward evening she tied a napkin around his neck and let him eat his fill of the dinner. Now as he sat at the table his head wobbled slowly from side to side and sometimes as he breathed there came from him a little worn-out grunt.

There was a stir in the café and Miss Amelia looked around quickly. Cousin Lymon had come in. The hunchback strutted into the café as he did every night, and when he reached the exact center of the room he stopped short and looked shrewdly around him, summing up the people and making a quick pattern of the emotional material at hand that night. The hunchback was a great mischief-maker. He enjoyed any kind of to-do, and without saying a word he could set the people at each other in a way that was miraculous. It was due to him that the Rainey twins had quarreled over a jacknife two years past, and had not spoken one word to each other since. He was present at the big fight between Rip Wellborn and Robert Calvert Hale, and every other fight for that matter since he had come into the town. He nosed around everywhere, knew the intimate business of everybody, and trespassed every waking hour. Yet, queerly enough, in spite of this it was the hunchback who was most responsible for the great popularity of the café. Things were never so gay as when he was around. When he walked into the room there was always a quick feeling of tension, because with this busybody about there was never any telling what might descend on you, or what might suddenly be brought to happen in the room. People are never so free with themselves and so recklessly glad as when there is some possibility of commotion or calamity ahead. So when the hunchback marched into the café everyone looked around at him and there was a quick outburst of talking and a drawing of corks.

Lymon waved his hand to Stumpy MacPhail who was sitting with Merlie Ryan and Henry Ford Crimp. 'I walked to Rotten Lake today to fish,' he said. 'And on the way I stepped over what appeared at first to be a big fallen tree. But then as I stepped over I felt something stir and I taken this second look and there I was straddling this here alligator long as from the front door to the kitchen and thicker than a hog.'

The hunchback chattered on. Everyone looked at him from time to time, and some kept track of his chattering and others did not. There were times when every word he said was nothing but lying and bragging. Nothing he said tonight was true. He had lain in bed with a summer quinsy all day long, and had only got up in the late afternoon in order to turn the ice-cream freezer. Everybody knew this, yet he stood there in the middle of the café and held forth with such lies and boasting that it was enough to shrivel the ears.

Miss Amelia watched him with her hands in her pockets and her head turned to one side. There was a softness about her gray, queer eyes and she was smiling gently to herself. Occasionally she glanced from the hunchback to the other people in the café—and then her look was proud, and there was in it the hint of a threat, as though daring anyone to try to hold him to account for all his foolery. Jeff was bringing in the suppers, already served on the plates, and the new electric fans in the café made a pleasant stir of coolness in the air.

'The little youngun is asleep,' said Henry Macy finally.

Miss Amelia looked down at the patient beside her, and composed her face for the matter in hand. The child's chin was resting on the table edge and a trickle of spit or Kroup Kure had bubbled from the corner of his mouth. His eyes were quite closed, and a little family of gnats had clustered peacefully in the corners. Miss Amelia put her hand on his head and shook it roughly, but the patient did not awake. So Miss Amelia lifted the child from the table, being careful not to touch the sore part of his leg, and went into the office. Henry Macy followed after her and they closed the office door.

Cousin Lymon was bored that evening. There was not much going on, and in spite of the heat the customers in the café were good-humored. Henry Ford Crimp and Horace Wells sat at the middle table with their arms around each other, sniggering over some long joke—but when he approached them he could make nothing of it as he had missed the beginning of the story. The moonlight brightened the dusty road, and the dwarfed peach trees were black and motionless: there was no breeze. The drowsy buzz of swamp mosquitoes was like an echo of the silent night. The town seemed dark, except far down the road to the right there was the flicker of a lamp. Somewhere in the darkness a woman sang in a high wild voice and the tune had no start and no finish and was made up of only three notes which went on and on and on. The hunchback stood leaning against the

41

banister of the porch, looking down the empty road as though hoping that someone would come along.

There were footsteps behind him, then a voice: 'Cousin Lymon, your dinner is set out upon the table.'

'My appetite is poor tonight,' said the hunchback, who had been eating sweet snuff all the day. 'There is a sourness in my mouth.'

'Just a pick,' said Miss Amelia. 'The breast, the liver, and the heart.'

Together they went back into the bright café, and sat down with Henry Macy. Their table was the largest one in the café, and on it there was a bouquet of swamp lilies in a Coca Cola bottle. Miss Amelia had finished with her patient and was satisfied with herself. From behind the closed office door there had come only a few sleepy whimpers, and before the patient could wake up and become terrified it was all over. The child was now slung across the shoulder of his father, sleeping deeply, his little arms dangling loose along his father's back, and his puffed-up face very red—they were leaving the café to go home.

Henry Macy was still silent. He ate carefully, making no noise when he swallowed, and was not a third as greedy as Cousin Lymon who had claimed to have no appetite and was now putting down helping after helping of the dinner. Occasionally Henry Macy looked across at Miss Amelia and again held his peace.

It was a typical Saturday night. An old couple who had come in from the country hesitated for a moment at the doorway, holding each other's hand, and finally decided to come inside. They had lived together so long, this old country couple, that they looked as similar as twins. They were brown, shriveled, and like two little walking peanuts. They left early, and by midnight most of the other customers were gone. Rosser Cline and Merlie Ryan still played checkers, and Stumpy MacPhail sat with a liquor bottle on his table (his wife would not allow it in the home) and carried on peaceable conversations with himself. Henry Macy had not yet gone away, and this was unusual, as he almost always went to bed soon after nightfall. Miss Amelia yawned sleepily, but Lymon was restless and she did not suggest that they close up for the night.

Finally, at one o'clock, Henry Macy looked up at the corner of the ceiling and said quietly to Miss Amelia: 'I got a letter today.'

Miss Amelia was not one to be impressed by this, because all sorts of business letters and catalogues came addressed to her.

'I got a letter from my brother,' said Henry Macy.

The hunchback, who had been goose-stepping about the café with his hands clasped behind his head, stopped suddenly. He was quick to sense any change in the atmosphere of a gathering. He glanced at each face in the room and waited.

Miss Amelia scowled and hardened her right fist. 'You are welcome to it,' she said.

'He is on parole. He is out of the penitentiary.'

The face of Miss Amelia was very dark, and she shivered although the night was warm. Stumpy Mac-Phail and Merlie Ryan pushed aside their checker game. The café was very quiet.

'Who?' asked Cousin Lymon. His large, pale ears seemed to grow on his head and stiffen. 'What?'

Miss Amelia slapped her hands palm down on the table. 'Because Marvin Macy is a——' But her voice hoarsened and after a few moments she only said: 'He belongs to be in that penitentiary the balance of his life.'

'What did he do?' asked Cousin Lymon.

There was a long pause, as no one knew exactly how to answer this. 'He robbed three filling stations,' said Stumpy MacPhail. But his words did not sound complete and there was a feeling of sins left unmentioned.

The hunchback was impatient. He could not bear to be left out of anything, even a great misery. The name Marvin Marcy was unknown to him, but it tantalized him as did any mention of subjects which others knew

43

about and of which he was ignorant—such as any reference to the old sawmill that had been torn down before he came, or a chance word about poor Morris Finestein, or the recollection of any event that had occurred before his time. Aside from this inborn curiosity, the hunchback took a great interest in robbers and crimes of all varieties. As he strutted around the table he was muttering the words 'released on parole' and 'penitentiary' to himself. But although he questioned insistently, he was unable to find anything, as nobody would dare to talk about Marvin Macy before Miss Amelia in the café.

'The letter did not say very much,' said Henry Macy. 'He did not say where he was going.'

'Humph!' said Amelia, and her face was still hardened and very dark. 'He will never set his split hoof on my premises. '

She pushed back her chair from the table, and made ready to close the café. Thinking about Marvin Macy may have set her to brooding, for she hauled the cash register back to the kitchen and put it in a private place. Henry Macy went off down the dark road. But Henry Ford Crimp and Merlie Ryan lingered for a time on the front porch. Later Merlie Ryan was to make certain claims, to swear that on that night he had a vision of what was to come. But the town paid no attention, for that was just the sort of thing that Merlie Ryan would claim. Miss Amelia and Cousin Lymon talked for a time in the parlor. And when at last the hunchback thought that he could sleep she arranged the mosquito netting over his bed and waited until he had finished with his prayers. Then she put on her long nightgown, smoked two pipes, and only after a long time went to sleep.

That autumn was a happy time. The crops around the countryside were good, and over at the Forks Falls market the price of tobacco held firm that year. After the long hot summer the first cool days had a clean bright sweetness. Goldenrod grew along the dusty roads, and the sugar cane was ripe and purple. The bus came each day from Cheehaw to carry off a few of the younger children to the consolidated school to get an education. Boys hunted foxes in the pinewoods, winter quilts were aired out on the wash lines, and sweet potatoes bedded in the ground with straw against the colder months to come. In the evening, delicate shreds of smoke rose from the chimneys, and the moon was round and orange in the autumn sky. There is no stillness like the quiet of the first cold nights in the fall. Sometimes, late in the night when there was no wind, there could be heard in the town the thin wild whistle of the train that goes through Society City on its way far off to the North.

For Miss Amelia Evans this was a time of great activity. She was at work from dawn until sundown. She made a new and bigger condenser for her still, and in one week ran off enough liquor to souse the whole county. Her old mule was dizzy from grinding so much sorghum, and she scalded her Mason jars and put away pear preserves. She was looking forward greatly to the first frost, because she had traded for three tremendous hogs, and intended to make much barbecue, chitterlins, and sausage.

During these weeks there was a quality about Miss Amelia that many people noticed. She laughed often, with a deep ringing laugh, and her whistling had a sassy, tuneful trickery. She was forever trying out her strength, lifting up heavy objects, or poking her tough biceps with her finger. One day she sat down to her typewriter and wrote a story—a story in which there were foreigners, trap doors, and millions of dollars. Cousin Lymon was with her always, traipsing along behind her coat-tails, and when she watched him her face had a bright, soft look, and when she spoke his name there lingered in her voice the undertone of love.

The first cold spell came at last. When Miss Amelia awoke one morning there were frost flowers on the windowpanes, and rime had silvered the patches of grass in the yard. Miss Amelia built a roaring fire in the kitchen stove, then went out of doors to judge the day. The air was cold and sharp, the sky pale green and cloudless. Very shortly people began to come in from the country to find out what Miss Amelia thought of the weather; she decided to kill the biggest hog, and word got round the countryside. The hog was slaughtered and a low oak fire started in the barbecue pit. There was the warm smell of pig blood and smoke in the back yard, the stamp of footsteps, the ring of voices in the winter air. Miss Amelia walked around giving orders and soon most of the work was done.

She had some particular business to do in Cheehaw that day, so after making sure that all was going well, she cranked up her car and got ready to leave. She asked Cousin Lymon to come with her, in fact, she asked him seven times, but he was loath to leave the commotion and wanted to remain. This seemed to trouble Miss Amelia, as she always liked to have him near to her, and was prone to be terribly homesick when she had to go any distance away. But after asking him seven times, she did not urge him any further. Before leaving she found a stick and drew a heavy line all around the barbecue pit, about two feet back from the edge, and told him not to trespass beyond that boundary. She left after dinner and intended to be back before dark.

Now, it is not so rare to have a truck or an automobile pass along the road and through the town on the way from Cheehaw to somewhere else. Every year the tax collector comes to argue with rich people such as Miss Amelia. And if somebody in the town, such as Merlie Ryan, takes a notion that he can connive to get a car on credit, or to pay down three dollars and have a fine electric icebox such as they advertise in the store windows of Cheehaw, then a city man will come out asking meddlesome questions, finding out all his troubles, and ruining his chances of buying anything on the installment plan. Sometimes, especially since they are working on the Forks Falls highway, the cars hauling the chain gang come through the town. And frequently people in automobiles get lost and stop to inquire how they can find the right road again. So, late that afternoon it was nothing unusual to have a truck pass the mill and stop in the middle of the road near the café of Miss Amelia. A man jumped down from the back of the truck, and the truck went on its way.

The man stood in the middle of the road and looked about him. He was a tall man, with brown curly hair, and slow-moving, deep-blue eyes. His lips were red and he smiled the lazy, half-mouthed smile of the braggart. The man wore a red shirt, and a wide belt of tooled leather; he carried a tin suitcase and a guitar. The first person in the town to see this newcomer was Cousin Lymon, who had heard the shifting gears and come around to investigate. The hunchback stuck his head around the corner of the porch, but did not step out altogether into full view. He and the man stared at each other, and it was not the look of two strangers meeting for the first time and swiftly summing up each other. It was a peculiar stare they exchanged between them, like the look of two criminals who recognize each other. Then the man in the red shirt shrugged his left shoulder and turned away. The face of the hunchback was very pale as he watched the man go down the road, and after a few moments he began to follow along carefully, keeping many paces away.

It was immediately known throughout the town that Marvin Macy had come back again. First, he went to the mill, propped his elbows lazily on a window sill and looked inside. He liked to watch others hard at work, as do all born loafers. The mill was thrown into a sort of numb confusion. The dyers left the hot vats, the spinners and weavers forgot about their machines, and even Stumpy MacPhail, who was foreman, did not know exactly what to do. Marvin Macy still smiled his wet half-mouthed smiles, and when he saw his brother, his bragging expression did not change. After looking over the mill Marvin Macy went down the road to the house where he had been raised, and left his suitcase and guitar on the front porch. Then he walked around

47

the millpond, looked over the church, the three stores, and the rest of the town. The hunchback trudged along quietly at some distance behind him, his hands in his pockets, and his little face still very pale.

It had grown late. The red winter sun was setting, and to the west the sky was deep gold and crimson. Ragged chimney swifts flew to their nests; lamps were lighted. Now and then there was the smell of smoke, and the warm rich odor of the barbecue slowly cooking in the pit behind the café. After making the rounds of the town Marvin Macy stopped before Miss Amelia's premises and read the sign above the porch. Then, not hesitating to trespass, he walked through the side yard. The mill whistle blew a thin, lonesome blast, and the day's shift was done. Soon there were others in Miss Amelia's back yard beside Marvin Macy—Henry Ford Crimp, Merlie Ryan, Stumpy MacPhail, and any number of children and people who stood around the edges of the property and looked on. Very little was said. Marvin Macy stood by himself on one side of the pit, and the rest of the people clustered together on the other side. Cousin Lymon stood somewhat apart from everyone, and he did not take his eyes from the face of Marvin Macy.

'Did you have a good time in the penitentiary?' asked Merlie Ryan, with a silly giggle.

Marvin Macy did not answer. He took from his hip pocket a large knife, opened it slowly, and honed the blade on the seat of his pants. Merlie Ryan grew suddenly very quiet and went to stand directly behind the broad back of Stumpy MacPhail.

Miss Amelia did not come home until almost dark. They heard the rattle of her automobile while she was still a long distance away, then the slam of the door and a bumping noise as though she were hauling something up the front steps of her premises. The sun had already set, and in the air there was the blue smoky glow of early winter evenings. Miss Amelia came down the back steps slowly, and the group in her yard waited very quietly. Few people in this world could stand up to Miss Amelia, and against Marvin Macy she had this special and bitter hate. Everyone waited to see her burst into a terrible holler, snatch up some dangerous object, and chase him altogether out of town. At first she did not see Marvin Macy, and her face had the relieved and dreamy expression that was natural to her when she reached home after having gone some distance away.

Miss Amelia must have seen Marvin Macy and Cousin Lymon at the same instant. She looked from one to the other, but it was not the wastrel from the penitentiary on whom she finally fixed her gaze of sick amazement. She, and everyone else, was looking at Cousin Lymon, and he was a sight to see.

The hunchback stood at the end of the pit, his pale face lighted by the soft glow from the smoldering oak fire. Cousin Lymon had a very peculiar accomplishment, which he used whenever he wished to ingratiate himself with someone. He would stand very still, and with just a little concentration, he could wiggle his large pale ears with marvelous quickness and ease. This trick he always used when he wanted to get something special out of Miss Amelia, and to her it was irresistible. Now as he stood there the hunchback's ears were wiggling furiously on his head, but it was not Miss Amelia at whom he was looking this time. The hunchback was smiling at Marvin Macy with an entreaty that was near to desperation. At first Marvin Macy paid no attention to him, and when he did finally glance at the hunchback it was without any appreciation whatsoever.

'What ails this Brokeback?' he asked with a rough jerk of his thumb.

No one answered. And Cousin Lymon, seeing that his accomplishment was getting him nowhere, added new efforts of persuasion. He fluttered his eyelids, so that they were like pale, trapped moths in his sockets. He scraped his feet around on the ground, waved his hands about, and finally began doing a little trotlike dance. In the last gloomy light of the winter afternoon he resembled the child of a swamphaunt.

Marvin Macy, alone of all the people in the yard, was unimpressed.

'Is the runt throwing a fit?' he asked, and when no one answered he stepped forward and gave Cousin Lymon a cuff on the side of his head. The hunchback staggered, then fell back on the ground. He sat where he had fallen, still looking up at Marvin Macy, and with great effort his ears managed one last forlorn little flap.

Now everyone turned to Miss Amelia to see what she would do. In all these years no one had so much as touched a hair of Cousin Lymon's head, although many had had the itch to do so. If anyone even spoke crossly to the hunchback, Miss Amelia would cut off this rash mortal's credit and find ways of making things go hard for him a long time afterward. So now if Miss Amelia had split open Marvin Macy's head with the ax on the back porch no one would have been surprised. But she did nothing of the kind.

There were times when Miss Amelia seemed to go into a sort of trance. And the cause of these trances was usually known and understood. For Miss Amelia was a fine doctor, and did not grind up swamp roots and other untried ingredients and give them to the first patient who came along; whenever she invented a new medicine she always tried it out first on herself. She would swallow an enormous dose and spend the following day walking thoughtfully back and forth from the café to the brick privy. Often, when there was a sudden keen gripe, she would stand quite still, her queer eyes staring down at the ground and her fists clenched; she was trying to decide which organ was being worked upon, and what misery the new medicine might be most likely to cure. And now as she watched the hunchback and Marvin Macy, her face wore this same expression, tense with reckoning some inward pain, although she had taken no new medicine that day.

'That will learn you, Brokeback,' said Marvin Macy.

Henry Macy pushed back his limp whitish hair from his forehead and coughed nervously. Stumpy MacPhail and Merlie Ryan shuffled their feet, and the children and black people on the outskirts of the property made not a sound. Marvin Macy folded the knife he had been honing, and after looking about him fearlessly he swaggered out of the yard. The embers in the pit were turning to gray feathery ashes and it was now quite dark.

That was the way Marvin Macy came back from the penitentiary. Not a living soul in all the town was glad to see him. Even Mrs. Mary Hale, who was a good woman and had raised him with love and care—at the first sight of him even this old foster mother dropped the skillet she was holding and burst into tears. But nothing could faze that Marvin Macy. He sat on the back steps of the Hale house, lazily picking his guitar, and when the supper was ready, he pushed the children of the household out of the way and served himself a big meal, although there had been barely enough hoecakes and white meat to go round. After eating he settled himself in the best and warmest sleeping place in the front room and was untroubled by dreams.

Miss Amelia did not open the café that night. She locked the doors and all the windows very carefully, nothing was seen of her and Cousin Lymon, and a lamp burned in her room all the night long.

Marvin Macy brought with him bad fortune, right from the first, as could be expected. The next day the weather turned suddenly, and it became hot. Even in the early morning there was a sticky sultriness in the atmosphere, the wind carried the rotten smell of the swamp, and delicate shrill mosquitoes webbed the green millpond. It was unseasonable, worst than August, and much damage was done. For nearly everyone in the county who owned a hog had copied Miss Amelia and slaughtered the day before. And what sausage could keep in such weather as this? After a few days there was everywhere the smell of slowly spoiling meat, and an atmosphere of dreary waste. Worse yet, a family reunion near the Forks Falls highway ate pork roast and died, every one of them. It was plain that their hog had been infected—and who could tell whether the rest of the meat was safe or not? People were torn between the longing for the good taste of pork, and the fear of death. It was a time of waste and confusion.

The cause of all this, Marvin Macy, had no shame in him. He was seen everywhere. During work hours he loafed about the mill, looking in at the windows, and on Sundays he dressed in his red shirt and paraded up and down the road with his guitar. He was still handsome—with his brown hair, his red lips, and his broad strong shoulders; but the evil in him was now too famous for his good looks to get him anywhere. And this evil was not measured only by the actual sins he had committed. True, he had robbed those filling stations. And before that he had ruined the tenderest girls in the county, and laughed about it. Any number of wicked things could be listed against him, but quite apart from these crimes there was about him a secret meanness that clung to him almost like a smell. Another thing—he never sweated, not even in August, and that surely is a sign worth pondering over.

Now it seemed to the town that he was more dangerous than he had ever been before, as in the penitentiary in Atlanta he must have learned the method of laying charms. Otherwise how could his effect on Cousin Lymon be explained? For since first setting eyes on Marvin Macy the hunchback was possessed by an unnatural spirit. Every minute he wanted to be following along behind this jailbird, and he was full of silly schemes to attract attention to himself. Still Marvin Macy either treated him hatefully or failed to notice him at all. Sometimes the hunchback would give up, perch himself on the banister of the front porch much as a sick bird huddles on a telephone wire, and grieve publicly.

'But why?' Miss Amelia would ask, staring at him with her crossed, gray eyes, and her fists closed tight.

'Oh, Marvin Macy,' groaned the hunchback, and the sound of the name was enough to upset the rhythm of his sobs so that he hiccuped. 'He has been to Atlanta.'

Miss Amelia would shake her head and her face was dark and hardened. To begin with she had no patience with any traveling; those who had made the trip to Atlanta or traveled fifty miles from home to see the ocean—those restless people she despised. 'Going to Atlanta does no credit to him.'

'He has been to the penitentiary,' said the hunchback, miserable with longing.

How are you going to argue against such envies as these? In her perplexity Miss Amelia did not herself sound any too sure of what she was saying. 'Been to the penitentiary, Cousin Lymon? Why, a trip like that is no travel to brag about.'

During these weeks Miss Amelia was closely watched by everyone. She went about absent-mindedly, her face remote as though she had lapsed into one of her gripe trances. For some reason, after the day of Marvin Macy's arrival, she put aside her overalls and wore always the red dress she had before this time reserved for Sundays, funerals, and sessions of the court. Then as the weeks passed she began to take some steps to clear up the situation. But her efforts were hard to understand. If it hurt her to see Cousin Lymon follow Marvin Macy about the town, why did she not make the issues clear once and for all, and tell the hunchback that if he had dealings with Marvin Macy she would turn him off the premises? That would have been simple, and Cousin Lymon would have had to submit to her, or else face the sorry business of finding himself loose in the world. But Miss Amelia seemed to have lost her will; for the first time in her life she hesitated as to just what course to pursue. And, like most people in such a position of uncertainty, she did the worst thing possible—she began following several courses at once, all of them contrary to each other.

The café was opened every night as usual, and, strangely enough, when Marvin Macy came swaggering through the door, with the hunchback at his heels, she did not turn him out. She even gave him free drinks and smiled at him in a wild, crooked way. At the same time she set a terrible trap for him out in the swamp that surely would have killed him if he had got caught. She let Cousin Lymon invite him to Sunday dinner, and then tried to trip him up as he went down the steps. She began a great campaign of pleasure for Cousin Lymon—making exhausting trips to various spectacles being held in distant places, driving the automobile thirty miles to a Chautauqua, taking him to Forks Falls to watch a parade. All in all it was a distracting time for Miss Amelia. In the opinion of most people she was well on her way in the climb up fools' hill, and everyone waited to see how it would all turn out.

The weather turned cold again, the winter was upon the town, and night came before the last shift in the mill was done. Children kept on all their garments when they slept, and women raised the backs of their skirts to toast themselves dreamily at the fire. After it rained, the mud in the road made hard frozen ruts, there were faint flickers of lamplight from the windows of the houses, the peach trees were scrawny and bare. In the dark, silent nights of winter-time the café was the warm center point of the town, the lights shining so brightly that they could be seen a quarter of a mile away. The great iron stove at the back of the room roared, crackled, and turned red. Miss Amelia had made red curtains for the windows, and from a salesman who passed through the town she bought a great bunch of paper roses that looked very real.

But it was not only the warmth, the decorations, and the brightness, that made the café what it was. There is a deeper reason why the café was so precious to this town. And this deeper reason has to do with a certain pride that had not hitherto been known in these parts. To understand this new pride the cheapness of human life must be kept in mind. There were always plenty of people clustered around a mill—but it was seldom that every family had enough meal, garments, and fat back to go the rounds. Life could become one long dim scramble just to get the things needed to keep alive. And the confusing point is this: All useful things have a price, and are bought only with money, as that is the way the world is run. You know without having to reason about it the price of a bale of cotton, or a quart of molasses. But no value has been put on human life; it is given to us free and taken without being paid for. What is it worth? If you look around, at times the value may seem to be little or nothing at all. Often after you have sweated and tried and things are not better for you, there comes a feeling deep down in the soul that you are not worth much.

But the new pride that the café brought to this town had an effect on almost everyone, even the children. For in order to come to the café you did not have to buy the dinner, or a portion of liquor. There were cold bottled drinks for a nickel. And if you could not even afford that, Miss Amelia had a drink called Cherry Juice which sold for a penny a glass, and was pink-colored and very sweet. Almost everyone, with the exception of Reverend T. M. Willin, came to the café at least once during the week. Children love to sleep in houses other than their own, and to eat at a neighbor's table; on such occasions they behave themselves decently and are proud. The people in the town were likewise proud when sitting at the tables in the café. They washed before coming to Miss Amelia's, and scraped their feet very politely on the threshold as they entered the café. There, for a few hours at least, the deep bitter knowing that you are not worth much in this world could be laid low.

The café was a special benefit to bachelors, unfortunate

people, and consumptives. And here it may be mentioned that there was some reason to suspect that Cousin Lymon was consumptive. The brightness of his gray eyes, his insistence, his talkativeness, and his cough—these were all signs. Besides, there is generally supposed to be some connection between a hunched spine and consumption. But whenever this subject had been mentioned to Miss Amelia she had become furious; she denied these symptoms with bitter vehemence, but on the sly she treated Cousin Lymon with hot chest platters, Kroup Kure, and such. Now this winter the hunchback's cough was worse, and sometimes even on cold days he would break out in a heavy sweat. But this did not prevent him from following along after Marvin Macy.

Early every morning he left the premises and went to the back door of Mrs. Hale's house, and waited and waited—as Marvin Macy was a lazy sleeper. He would stand there and call out softly. His voice was just like the voices of children who squat patiently over those tiny little holes in the ground where doodlebugs are thought to live, poking the hole with a broom straw, and calling plaintively: 'Doodlebug, Doodlebug—fly away home. Mrs. Doodlebug, Mrs. Doodlebug. Come out, come out. Your house is on fire and all your children are burning up.' In just such a voice—at once sad, luring, and resigned—would the hunchback call Marvin Macy's name each morning. Then when Marvin Macy came out for the day, he would trail him about the town, and sometimes they would be gone for hours together out in the swamp.

And Miss Amelia continued to do the worst thing possible: that is, to try to follow several courses at once. When Cousin Lymon left the house she did not call him back, but only stood in the middle of the road and watched lonesomely until he was out of sight. Nearly every day Marvin Macy turned up with Cousin Lymon at dinnertime, and ate at her table. Miss Amelia opened the pear preserves, and the table was well-set with ham or chicken, great bowls of hominy grits, and winter peas.

It is true that on one occasion Miss Amelia tried to poison Marvin Macy—but there was a mistake, the plates were confused, and it was she herself who got the poisoned dish. This she quickly realized by the slight bitterness of the food, and that day she ate no dinner. She sat tilted back in her chair, feeling her muscle, and looking at Marvin Macy.

Every night Marvin Macy came to the café and settled himself at the best and largest table, the one in the center of the room. Cousin Lymon brought him liquor, for which he did not pay a cent. Marvin Macy brushed the hunchback aside as if he were a swamp mosquito, and not only did he show no gratitude for these favors, but if the hunchback got in his way he would cuff him with the back of his hand, or say: 'Out of my way, Brokeback —I'll snatch you bald-headed.' When this happened Miss Amelia would come out from behind her counter and approach Marvin Macy very slowly, her fists clenched, her peculiar red dress hanging awkwardly around her bony knees. Marvin Macy would also clench his fists and they would walk slowly and meaningfully around each other. But, although everyone watched breathlessly, nothing ever came of it. The time for the fight was not yet ready.

There is one particular reason why this winter is remembered and still talked about. A great thing happened. People woke up on the second of January and found the whole world about them altogether changed. Little ignorant children looked out of the windows, and they were so puzzled that they began to cry. Old people harked back and could remember nothing in these parts to equal the phenomenon. For in the night it had snowed. In the dark hours after midnight the dim flakes started falling softly on the town. By dawn the ground was covered, and the strange snow banked the ruby windows of the church, and whitened the roofs of the houses. The snow gave the town a drawn, bleak look. The two-room houses near the mill were dirty, crooked, and seemed about to collapse, and somehow everything was

dark and shrunken. But the snow itself—there was a
beauty about it few people around here had ever known
before. The snow was not white, as Northerners had
pictured it to be; in the snow there were soft colors of
blue and silver, the sky was a gentle shining gray. And
the dreamy quietness of falling snow—when had the town
been so silent?

People reacted to the snowfall in various ways. Miss
Amelia, on looking out of her window, thoughtfully
wiggled the toes of her bare foot, gathered close to her
neck the collar of her nightgown. She stood there for
some time, then commenced to draw the shutters and
lock every window on the premises. She closed the place
completely, lighted the lamps, and sat solemnly over her
bowl of grits. The reason for this was not that Miss
Amelia feared the snowfall. It was simply that she was
unable to form an immediate opinion of this new event,
and unless she knew exactly and definitely what she
thought of a matter (which was nearly always the case)
she preferred to ignore it. Snow had never fallen in this
county in her lifetime, and she had never thought about
it one way or the other. But if she admitted this snowfall she would have to come to some decision, and in
those days there was enough distraction in her life as it
was already. So she poked about the gloomy, lamp-
lighted house and pretended that nothing had happened.
Cousin Lymon, on the contrary, chased around in the
wildest excitement, and when Miss Amelia turned her
back to dish him some breakfast he slipped out of the
door.

Marvin Macy laid claim to the snowfall. He said that
he knew snow, had seen it in Atlanta, and from the way
he walked about the town that day it was as though he
owned every flake. He sneered at the little children who
crept timidly out of the houses and scooped up handfuls
of snow to taste. Reverend Willin hurried down the road
with a furious face, as he was thinking deeply and trying
to weave the snow into his Sunday sermon. Most people
were humble and glad about this marvel; they spoke in

hushed voices and said 'thank you' and 'please' more than was necessary. A few weak characters, of course, were demoralized and got drunk—but they were not numerous. To everyone this was an occasion and many counted their money and planned to go to the café that night.

Cousin Lymon followed Marvin Macy about all day, seconding his claim to the snow. He marveled that snow did not fall as does rain, and stared up at the dreamy, gently falling flakes until he stumbled from dizziness. And the pride he took on himself, basking in the glory of Marvin Macy—it was such that many people could not resist calling out to him: ' "Oho," said the fly on the chariot wheel. "What a dust we do raise." '

Miss Amelia did not intend to serve dinner. But when, at six o'clock, there was the sound of footsteps on the porch she opened the front door cautiously. It was Henry Ford Crimp, and though there was no food, she let him sit at a table and served him a drink. Others came. The evening was blue, bitter, and though the snow fell no longer there was a wind from the pine trees that swept up delicate flurries from the ground. Cousin Lymon did not come until after dark, with him Marvin Macy, and he carried his tin suitcase and his guitar.

'So you mean to travel?' said Miss Amelia quickly.

Marvin Macy warmed himself at the stove. Then he settled down at his table and carefully sharpened a little stick. He picked his teeth, frequently taking the stick out of his mouth to look at the end and wipe it on the sleeve of his coat. He did not bother to answer.

The hunchback looked at Miss Amelia, who was behind the counter. His face was not in the least beseeching; he seemed quite sure of himself. He folded his hands behind his back and perked up his ears confidently. His cheeks were red, his eyes shining, and his clothes were soggy wet. 'Marvin Macy is going to visit a spell with us,' he said.

Miss Amelia made no protest. She only came out from behind the counter and hovered over the stove, as though the news had made her suddenly cold. She did not warm

59

her backside modestly, lifting her skirt only an inch or so, as do most women when in public. There was not a grain of modesty about Miss Amelia, and she frequently seemed to forget altogether that there were men in the room. Now as she stood warming herself, her red dress was pulled up quite high in the back so that a piece of her strong, hairy thigh could be seen by anyone who cared to look at it. Her head was turned to one side, and she had begun talking with herself, nodding and wrinkling her forehead, and there was the tone of accusation and reproach in her voice although the words were not plain. Meanwhile, the hunchback and Marvin Macy had gone upstairs—up to the parlor with the pampas grass and the two sewing machines, to the private rooms where Miss Amelia had lived the whole of her life. Down in the café you could hear them bumping around, unpacking Marvin Macy, and getting him settled.

That is the way Marvin Macy crowded into Miss Amelia's home. At first Cousin Lymon, who had given Marvin Macy his own room, slept on the sofa in the parlor. But the snowfall had a bad effect on him; he caught a cold that turned into a winter quinsy, so Miss Amelia gave up her bed to him. The sofa in the parlor was much too short for her, her feet lapped over the edges, and often she rolled off onto the floor. Perhaps it was this lack of sleep that clouded her wits; everything she tried to do against Marvin Macy rebounded on herself. She got caught in her own tricks, and found herself in many pitiful positions. But still she did not put Marvin Macy off the premises, as she was afraid that she would be left alone. Once you have lived with another, it is a great torture to have to live alone. The silence of a firelit room when suddenly the clock stops ticking, the nervous shadows in an empty house—it is better to take in your mortal enemy than face the terror of living alone.

The snow did not last. The sun came out and within two days the town was just as it had always been before. Miss Amelia did not open her house until every flake had melted. Then she had a big house cleaning and aired everything out in the sun. But before that, the very first thing she did on going out again into her yard, was to tie a rope to the largest branch of the chinaberry tree. At the end of the rope she tied a crocus sack tightly stuffed with sand. This was the punching bag she made for herself and from that day on she would box with it out in her yard every morning. Already she was a fine fighter—a little heavy on her feet, but knowing all manner of mean holds and squeezes to make up for this.

Miss Amelia, as has been mentioned, measured six feet two inches in height. Marvin Macy was one inch shorter. In weight they were about even—both of them weighing close to a hundred and sixty pounds. Marvin Macy had the advantage in slyness of movement, and in toughness of chest. In fact from the outward point of view the odds were altogether in his favor. Yet almost everybody in the town was betting on Miss Amelia; scarcely a person would put up money on Marvin Macy. The town remembered the great fight between Miss Amelia and a Fork Falls lawyer who had tried to cheat her. He had been a huge strapping fellow, but he was left three-quarters dead when she had finished with him. And it was not only her talent as a boxer that had impressed everyone—she could demoralize her enemy by making terrifying faces and fierce noises, so that even the spectators were sometimes cowed. She was brave, she practiced faithfully with her punching bag, and in this case she was clearly in the right. So people had confidence in her, and they waited. Of course there was no set date for this fight. There were just the signs that were too plain to be overlooked.

During these times the hunchback strutted around with a pleased little pinched-up face. In many delicate and clever ways he stirred up trouble between them. He was constantly plucking at Marvin Macy's trouser leg to draw attention to himself. Sometimes he followed in Miss Amelia's footsteps—but these days it was only in order to imitate her awkward long-legged walk; he crossed his eyes and aped her gestures in a way that made her appear to be a freak. There was something so terrible about this that even the silliest customers of the café, such as Merlie Ryan, did not laugh. Only Marvin Macy drew up the left corner of his mouth and chuckled. Miss Amelia, when this happened, would be divided between two emotions. She would look at the hunchback with a lost, dismal reproach—then turn toward Marvin Macy with her teeth clamped.

'Bust a gut!' she would say bitterly.

And Marvin Macy, most likely, would pick up the guitar from the floor beside his chair. His voice was wet and slimy, as he always had too much spit in his mouth. And the tunes he sang glided slowly from his throat like eels. His strong fingers picked the strings with dainty skill, and everything he sang both lured and exasperated. This was usually more than Miss Amelia could stand.

'Bust a gut!' she would repeat, in a shout.

But always Marvin Macy had the answer ready for her. He would cover the strings to silence the quivering leftover tones, and reply with slow, sure insolence.

'Everything you holler at me bounces back on yourself. Yah! Yah!'

Miss Amelia would have to stand there helpless, as no one has ever invented a way out of this trap. She could not shout out abuse that would bounce back on herself. He had the best of her, there was nothing she could do.

So things went on like this. What happened between the three of them during the nights in the rooms upstairs nobody knows. But the café became more and more crowded every night. A new table had to be brought in. Even the Hermit, the crazy man named Rainer Smith, who took to the swamps years ago, heard something of the situation and came one night to look in at the window and brood over the gathering in the bright café. And the climax each evening was the time when Miss Amelia and Marvin Macy doubled their fists, squared up, and glared at each other. Usually this did not happen after any especial argument, but it seemed to come about mysteriously, by means of some instinct on the part of both of them. At these times the café would become so quiet that you could hear the bouquet of paper roses rustling in the draft. And each night they held this fighting stance a little longer than the night before.

The fight took place on Ground Hog Day, which is the second of February. The weather was favorable, being neither rainy nor sunny, and with a neutral temperature. There were several signs that this was the appointed day, and by ten o'clock the news spread all over the county. Early in the morning Miss Amelia went out and cut down her punching bag. Marvin Macy sat on the back step with a tin can of hog fat between his knees and carefully greased his arms and his legs. A hawk with a bloody breast flew over the town and circled twice around the property of Miss Amelia. The tables in the café were moved out to the back porch, so that the whole big room was cleared for the fight. There was every sign. Both Miss Amelia and Marvin Macy ate four helpings of half-raw roast for dinner, and then lay down in the afternoon to store up strength. Marvin Macy rested in the big room upstairs, while Miss Amelia stretched herself out on the bench in her office. It was plain from her white stiff face what a torment it was for her to be lying still and doing nothing, but she lay there quiet as a corpse with her eyes closed and her hands crossed on her chest.

Cousin Lymon had a restless day, and his little face was drawn and tightened with excitement. He put himself up a lunch, and set out to find the ground hog—within an hour he returned, the lunch eaten, and said that the ground hog had seen his shadow and there was to be bad weather ahead. Then, as Miss Amelia and Marvin Macy were both resting to gather strength, and he was left to himself, it occurred to him that he might as well paint the front porch. The house had not been painted for years—in fact, God knows if it had ever been painted at all. Cousin Lymon scrambled around, and soon he had painted half the floor of the porch a gay bright green. It was a loblolly job, and he smeared himself all over. Typically enough he did not even finish the floor, but changed over to the walls, painting as high as he could reach and then standing on a crate to get up a foot higher. When the paint ran out, the right side of the floor was bright green and there was a jagged portion of wall that had been painted. Cousin Lymon left it at that.

There was something childish about his satisfaction with his painting. And in this respect a curious fact should be mentioned. No one in the town, not even Miss Amelia, had any idea how old the hunchback was. Some maintained that when he came to town he was about twelve years old, still a child—others were certain that he was well past forty. His eyes were blue and steady as a child's but there were lavender crêpy shadows beneath these blue eyes that hinted of age. It was impossible to guess his age by his hunched queer body. And even his teeth gave no clue—they were all still in his head (two were broken from cracking a pecan), but he had stained them with so much sweet snuff that it was impossible to decide whether they were old teeth or young teeth. When questioned directly about his age the hunchback professed to know absolutely nothing—he had no idea how long he had been on the earth, whether for ten years or a hundred! So his age remained a puzzle.

Cousin Lymon finished his painting at five-thirty o'clock in the afternoon. The day had turned colder and there was a wet taste in the air. The wind came up from the pinewoods, rattling windows, blowing an old newspaper down the road until at last it caught upon a thorn tree. People began to come in from the country; packed automobiles that bristled with the poked-out heads of children, wagons drawn by old mules who seemed to smile in a weary, sour way and plodded along with their tired eyes half-closed. Three young boys came from Society City. All three of them wore yellow rayon shirts and caps put on backward—they were as much alike as triplets, and could always be seen at cock fights and camp meetings. At six o'clock the mill whistle sounded the end of the day's shift and the crowd was complete. Naturally, among the newcomers there were some riffraff, unknown characters, and so forth—but even so the gathering was quiet. A hush was on the town and the faces of people were strange in the fading light. Darkness hovered softly; for a moment the sky was a pale clear yellow against which the gables of the church stood out in dark and bare outline, then the sky died slowly and the darkness gathered into night.

Seven is a popular number, and especially it was a favorite with Miss Amelia. Seven swallows of water for hiccups, seven runs around the millpond for cricks in the neck, seven doses of Amelia Miracle Mover as a worm cure—her treatment nearly always hinged on this number. It is a number of mingled possibilities, and all who love mystery and charms set store by it. So the fight was to take place at seven o'clock. This was known to everyone, not by announcement or words, but understood in the unquestioning way that rain is understood, or an evil odor from the swamp. So before seven o'clock everyone gathered gravely around the property of Miss Amelia. The cleverest got into the café itself and stood lining the walls of the room. Others crowded onto the front porch, or took a stand in the yard.

Miss Amelia and Marvin Macy had not yet shown themselves. Miss Amelia, after resting all afternoon on the office bench, had gone upstairs. On the other hand Cousin Lymon was at your elbow every minute, threading his way through the crowd, snapping his fingers nervously, and batting his eyes. At one minute to seven o'clock he squirmed his way into the café and climbed up on the counter. All was very quiet.

It must have been arranged in some manner beforehand. For just at the stroke of seven Miss Amelia showed herself at the head of the stairs. At the same instant Marvin Macy appeared in front of the café and the crowd made way for him silently. They walked toward each other with no haste, their fists already gripped, and their eyes like the eyes of dreamers. Miss Amelia had changed her red dress for her old overalls, and they were rolled up to the kness. She was barefooted and she had an iron strengthband around her right wrist. Marvin Macy had also rolled his trouser legs—he was naked to the waist and heavily greased; he wore the heavy shoes that had been issued him when he left the penitentiary. Stumpy MacPhail stepped forward from the crowd and slapped their hip pockets with the palm of his right hand to make sure there would be no sudden knives. Then they were alone in the cleared center of the bright café.

There was no signal, but they both struck out simultaneously. Both blows landed on the chin, so that the heads of Miss Amelia and Marvin Macy bobbed back and they were left a little groggy. For a few seconds after the first blows they merely shuffled their feet around on the bare floor, experimenting with various positions, and making mock fists. Then, like wildcats, they were suddenly on each other. There was the sound of knocks, panting, and thumpings on the floor. They were so fast that it was hard to take in what was going on—but once Miss Amelia was hurled backward so that she staggered and almost fell, and another time Marvin Macy caught a knock on the shoulder that spun him around like a top. So the fight went on in this wild violent way with no sign of weakening on either side.

During a struggle like this, when the enemies are as quick and strong as these two, it is worth-while to turn from the confusion of the fight itself and observe the spectators. The people had flattened back as close as possible against the walls. Stumpy MacPhail was in a corner, crouched over and with his fists tight in sympathy, making strange noises. Poor Merlie Ryan had his mouth so wide open that a fly buzzed into it, and was swallowed before Merlie realized what had happened. And Cousin

Lymon—he was worth watching. The hunchback still stood on the counter, so that he was raised up above everyone else in the café. He had his hands on his hips, his big head thrust forward, and his little legs bent so that the knees jutted outward. The excitement had made him break out in a rash, and his pale mouth shivered.

Perhaps it was half an hour before the course of the fight shifted. Hundreds of blows had been exchanged, and there was still a deadlock. Then suddenly Marvin Macy managed to catch hold of Miss Amelia's left arm and pinion it behind her back. She struggled and got a grasp around his waist; the real fight was now begun. Wrestling is the natural way of fighting in this county— as boxing is too quick and requires much thinking and concentration. And now that Miss Amelia and Marvin were locked in a hold together the crowd came out of its daze and pressed in closer. For a while the fighters grappled muscle to muscle, their hipbones braced against each other. Backward and forward, from side to side, they swayed in this way. Marvin Macy still had not sweated, but Miss Amelia's overalls were drenched and so much sweat had trickled down her legs that she left wet footprints on the floor. Now the test had come, and in these moments of terrible effort, it was Miss Amelia who was the stronger. Marvin Macy was greased and slippery, tricky to grasp, but she was stronger. Gradually she bent him over backward, and inch by inch she forced him to the floor. It was a terrible thing to watch and their deep hoarse breaths were the only sound in the café. At last she had him down, and straddled; her strong big hands were on his throat.

But at that instant, just as the fight was won, a cry sounded in the café that caused a shrill bright shiver to run down the spine. And what took place has been a mystery ever since. The whole town was there to testify what happened, but there were those who doubted their own eyesight. For the counter on which Cousin Lymon stood was at least twelve feet from the fighters in the center of the café. Yet at the instant Miss Amelia grasped the throat of Marvin Macy the hunchback sprang forward and sailed through the air as though he had grown hawk wings. He landed on the broad strong back of Miss Amelia and clutched at her neck with his clawed little fingers.

The rest is confusion. Miss Amelia was beaten before the crowd could come to their senses. Because of the hunchback the fight was won by Marvin Macy, and at the end Miss Amelia lay sprawled on the floor, her arms flung outward and motionless. Marvin Macy stood over her, his face somewhat popeyed, but smiling his old half-mouthed smile. And the hunchback, he had suddenly disappeared. Perhaps he was frightened about what he had done, or maybe he was so delighted that he wanted to glory with himself alone—at any rate he slipped out of the café and crawled under the back steps. Someone poured water on Miss Amelia, and after a time she got up slowly and dragged herself into her office. Through the open door the crowd could see her sitting at her desk, her head in the crook of her arm, and she was sobbing with the last of her grating, winded breath. Once she gathered her right fist together and knock it three times on the top of her office desk, then her hand opened feebly and lay palm upward and still. Stumpy MacPhail stepped forward and closed the door.

The crowd was quiet, and one by one the people left the café. Mules were waked up and untied, automobiles cranked, and the three boys from Society City roamed off down the road on foot. This was not a fight to hash over and talk about afterward; people went home and pulled the covers up over their heads. The town was dark, except for the premises of Miss Amelia, but every room was lighted there the whole night long.

Marvin Macy and the hunchback must have left the town an hour or so before daylight. And before they went away this is what they did:

They unlocked the private cabinet of curios and took everything in it.

They broke the mechanical piano.

They carved terrible words on the café tables.

They found the watch that opened in the back to show a picture of a waterfall and took that also.

They poured a gallon of sorghum syrup all over the kitchen floor and smashed the jars of preserves.

They went out in the swamp and completely wrecked the still, ruining the big new condenser and the cooler, and setting fire to the shack itself.

They fixed a dish of Miss Amelia's favorite food, grits with sausage, seasoned it with enough poison to kill off the county, and placed this dish temptingly on the café counter.

They did everything ruinous they could think of without actually breaking into the office where Miss Amelia stayed the night. Then they went off together, the two of them.

That was how Miss Amelia was left alone in the town. The people would have helped her if they had known how, as people in this town will as often as not be kindly if they have a chance. Several housewives nosed around with brooms and offered to clear up the wreck. But Miss Amelia only looked at them with lost crossed eyes and shook her head. Stumpy MacPhail came in on the third day to buy a plug of Queenie tobacco, and Miss Amelia said the price was one dollar. Everything in the café had suddenly risen in price to be worth one dollar. And what sort of a café is that? Also, she changed very queerly as a doctor. In all the years before she had been much more popular than the Cheehaw doctor. She had never monkeyed with a patient's soul, taking away from him such real necessities as liquor, tobacco, and so forth. Once in a great while she might carefully warn a patient never to eat fried watermelon or some such dish it had never occurred to a person to want in the first place. Now all this wise doctoring was over. She told one-half of her patients that they were going to die outright, and to the remaining half she recommended cures so far-fetched and agonizing that no one in his right mind would consider them for a moment.

Miss Amelia let her hair grow ragged, and it was turning gray. Her face lengthened, and the great muscles of her body shrank until she was thin as old maids are thin when they go crazy. And those gray eyes—slowly day by day they were more crossed, and it was as though they sought each other out to exchange a little glance of grief and lonely recognition. She was not pleasant to listen to; her tongue had sharpened terribly.

When anyone mentioned the hunchback she would say only this: 'Ho! if I could lay hand to him I would rip out his gizzard and throw it to the cat!' But it was not so much the words that were terrible, but the voice in which they were said. Her voice had lost its old vigor; there was none of the ring of vengeance it used to have when she would mention 'that loom-fixer I was married to,' or some other enemy. Her voice was broken, soft, and sad as the wheezy whine of the church pump-organ.

For three years she sat out on the front steps every night, alone and silent, looking down the road and waiting. But the hunchback never returned. There were rumors that Marvin Macy used him to climb into windows and steal, and other rumors that Marvin Macy had sold him into a side show. But both these reports were traced back to Merlie Ryan. Nothing true was ever heard of him. It was in the fourth year that Miss Amelia hired a Cheehaw carpenter and had him board up the premises, and there in those closed rooms she has remained ever since.

Yes, the town is dreary. On August afternoons the road is empty, white with dust, and the sky above is bright as glass. Nothing moves—there are no children's voices, only the hum of the mill. The peach trees seem to grow more crooked every summer, and the leaves are dull gray and of a sickly delicacy. The house of Miss Amelia leans so much to the right that it is now only a question of time when it will collapse completely, and people are careful not to walk around the yard. There is no good liquor to be bought in the town; the nearest still is eight miles away, and the liquor is such that those who drink it grow warts on their livers the size of goobers, and dream themselves into a dangerous inward world. There is absolutely nothing to do in the town. Walk around the millpond, stand kicking at a rotten stump, figure out what you can do with the old wagon wheel by the side of the road near the church. The soul rots with boredom. You might as well go down to the Forks Falls highway and listen to the chain gang.

THE TWELVE MORTAL MEN

The Forks Falls highway is three miles from the town, and it is here the chain gang has been working. The road is of macadam, and the county decided to patch up the rough places and widen it at a certain dangerous place. The gang is made up of twelve men, all wearing black and white striped prison suits, and chained at the ankles. There is a guard, with a gun, his eyes drawn to red slits by the glare. The gang works all the day long, arriving huddled in the prison cart soon after daybreak, and being driven off again in the gray August twilight. All day there is the sound of the picks striking into the clay earth, hard sunlight, the smell of sweat. And every day there is music. One dark voice will start a phrase, half-sung, and like a question. And after a moment another voice will join in, soon the whole gang will be singing. The voices are dark in the golden glare, the music intricately blended, both somber and joyful. The music will swell until at last it seems that the sound does not come from the twelve men on the gang, but from the earth itself, or the wide sky. It is music that causes the heart to broaden and the listener to grow cold with ecstasy and fright. Then slowly the music will sink down until at last there remains one lonely voice, then a great hoarse breath, the sun, the sound of the picks in the silence.

And what kind of gang is this that can make such music? Just twelve mortal men, seven of them black and five of them white boys from this county. Just twelve mortal men who are together.

Wunderkind

Wunderkind

S HE CAME into the living room, her music satchel plopping against her winter-stockinged legs and her other arm weighted down with school books, and stood for a moment listening to the sounds from the studio. A soft procession of piano chords and the tuning of a violin. Then Mister Bilderbach called out to her in his chunky, guttural tones:

'That you, Bienchen?'

As she jerked off her mittens she saw that her fingers were twitching to the motions of the fugue she had practiced that morning. 'Yes,' she answered. 'It's me.'

'I,' the voice corrected. 'Just a moment.'

She could hear Mister Lafkowitz talking—his words spun out in a silky, unintelligible hum. A voice almost like a woman's, she thought, compared to Mister Bilderbach's. Restlessness scattered her attention. She fumbled with her geometry book and *Le Voyage de Monsieur Perrichon* before putting them on the table. She sat down on the sofa and began to take her music from the satchel. Again she saw her hands—the quivering tendons that stretched down from her knuckles, the sore finger tip capped with curled, dingy tape. The sight sharpened the fear that had begun to torment her for the past few months.

Noiselessly she mumbled a few phrases of encouragement to herself. A good lesson—a good lesson—like it used to be— Her lips closed as she heard the stolid sound of Mister Bilderbach's footsteps across the floor of the studio and the creaking of the door as it slid open.

For a moment she had the peculiar feeling that during most of the fifteen years of her life she had been looking at the face and shoulders that jutted from behind the door, in a silence disturbed only by the muted, blank plucking of a violin string. Mister Bilderbach. Her teacher, Mr. Bilderbach. The quick eyes behind the horn-rimmed glasses; the light, thin hair and the narrow face beneath; the lips full and loose shut and the lower one pink and shining from the bites of his teeth; the forked veins in his temples throbbing plainly enough to be observed across the room.

'Aren't you a little early?' he asked, glancing at the clock on the mantelpiece that had pointed to five minutes of twelve for a month. 'Josef's in here. We're running over a little sonatino by someone he knows.'

'Good,' she said, trying to smile. 'I'll listen.' She could see her fingers sinking powerless into a blur of piano keys. She felt tired—felt that if he looked at her much longer her hands might tremble.

He stood uncertain, halfway in the room. Sharply his teeth pushed down on his bright, swollen lips. 'Hungry, Bienchen?' he asked. 'There's some apple cake Anna made, and milk.'

'I'll wait till afterward,' she said. 'Thanks.'

'After you finish with a very fine lesson—eh?' His smile seemed to crumble at the corners.

There was a sound from behind him in the studio and Mister Lafkowitz pushed at the other panel of the door and stood beside him.

'Frances?' he said, smiling. 'And how is the work coming now?'

Without meaning to, Mister Lafkowitz always made her feel clumsy and overgrown. He was such a small man himself, with a weary look when he was not holding his violin. His eyebrows curved high above his sallow, Jewish face as though asking a question, but the lids of his eyes drowsed languorous and indifferent. Today he seemed distracted. She watched him come into the room for no apparent purpose, holding his pearl-tipped bow in his still fingers, slowly gliding the white horse-hair through a chalky piece of rosin. His eyes were sharp bright slits today and the linen handkerchief that flowed down from his collar darkened the shadows beneath them.

'I gather you're doing a lot now,' smiled Mister Lafkowitz, although she had not yet answered the question.

She looked at Mister Bilderbach. He turned away. His heavy shoulders pushed the door open wide so that the late afternoon sun came through the window of the studio and shafted yellow over the dusty living room. Behind her teacher she could see the squat long piano, the window, and the bust of Brahms.

'No,' she said to Mister Lafkowitz, 'I'm doing terribly.' Her thin fingers flipped at the pages of her music. 'I don't know what's the matter,' she said, looking at Mister Bilderbach's stooped muscular back that stood tense and listening.

Mister Lafkowitz smiled. 'There are times, I suppose, when one——'

A harsh chord sounded from the piano. 'Don't you think we'd better get on with this?' asked Mister Bilderbach.

'Immediately,' said Mister Lafkowitz, giving the bow one more scrape before starting toward the door. She could see him pick up his violin from the top of the piano. He caught her eye and lowered the instrument. 'You've seen the picture of Heime?'

Her fingers curled tight over the sharp corner of the satchel. 'What picture?'

'One of Heime in the *Musical Courier* there on the table. Inside the top cover.'

The sonatina began. Discordant yet somehow simple. Empty but with a sharp-cut style of its own. She reached for the magazine and opened it.

There Heime was—in the left-hand corner. Holding his violin with his fingers hooked down over the strings for a pizzicato. With his dark serge knickers strapped neatly beneath his knees, a sweater and rolled collar. It was a bad picture. Although it was snapped in profile his eyes were cut around toward the photographer and his finger looked as though it would pluck the wrong string. He seemed suffering to turn around toward the picture-taking apparatus. He was thinner—his stomach did not poke out now—but he hadn't changed much in six months.

Heime Israelsky, talented young violinist, snapped while at work in his teacher's studio on Riverside Drive. Young Master Israelsky, who will soon celebrate his fifteenth birthday, has been invited to play the Beethoven Concerto with—

That morning, after she had practiced from six until eight, her dad had made her sit down at the table with the family for breakfast. She hated breakfast; it gave her a sick feeling afterward. She would rather wait and get four chocolate bars with her twenty cents lunch money and munch them during school—bringing up little morsels from the pocket under cover of her handkerchief, stopping dead when the silver paper rattled. But this morning her dad had put a fried egg on her plate and she had known that if it burst—so that the slimy yellow oozed over the white—she would cry. And that had happened. The same feeling was upon her now. Gingerly she laid the magazine back on the table and closed her eyes.

The music in the studio seemed to be urging violently and clumsily for something that was not to be had. After a moment her thoughts drew back from Heime and the concerto and the picture—and hovered around the lesson once more. She slid over on the sofa until she could see plainly into the studio—the two of them playing, peering at the notations on the piano, lustfully drawing out all that was there.

She could not forget the memory of Mister Bilderbach's face as he had stared at her a moment ago. Her hands, still twitching unconsciously to the motions of the fugue, closed over her bony knees. Tired, she was. And with a circling, sinking away feeling like the one that often came to her just before she dropped off to sleep on the nights when she had over-practiced. Like those weary half-dreams that buzzed and carried her out into their own whirligig space.

A *Wunderkind*—a *Wunderkind*—a *Wunderkind*. The syllables would come out rolling in the deep German way, roar against her ears and then fall to a murmur. Along with the faces circling, swelling out in distortion, diminishing to pale blobs—Mister Bilderbach, Mrs. Bilderbach, Heime, Mister Lafkowitz. Around and around in a circle revolving to the guttural *Wunderkind*. Mister Bilderbach looming large in the middle of the circle, his face urging—with the others around him.

Phrases of music seesawing crazily. Notes she had been practicing falling over each other like a handful of marbles dropped downstairs. Bach, Debussy, Prokofieff, Brahms—timed grotesquely to the far off throb of her tired body and the buzzing circle.

Sometimes—when she had not worked more than three hours or had stayed out from high school—the dreams were not so confused. The music soared clearly in her mind and quick, precise little memories would come back —clear as the sissy 'Age of Innocence' picture Heime had given her after their joint concert was over.

A *Wunderkind*—a *Wunderkind*. That was what Mister Bilderbach had called her when, at twelve, she first came to him. Older pupils had repeated the word.

Not that he had ever said the word to her. 'Bienchen—' (She had a plain American name but he never used it except when her mistakes were enormous.) 'Bienchen,' he would say, 'I know it must be terrible. Carrying around all the time a head that thick. Poor Bienchen——'

Mister Bilderbach's father had been a Dutch violinist. His mother was from Prague. He had been born in this country and had spent his youth in Germany. So many times she wished she had not been born and brought up in just Cincinnati. How do you say *cheese* in German? Mister Bilderbach, what is Dutch for *I don't understand you?*

The first day she came to the studio. After she played the whole Second Hungarian Rhapsody from memory. The room graying with twilight. His face as he leaned over the piano.

'Now we begin all over,' he said that first day. 'It—playing music—is more than cleverness. If a twelve-year-old girl's fingers cover so many keys to a second—that means nothing.'

He tapped his broad chest and his forehead with his stubby hand. 'Here and here. You are old enough to understand that.' He lighted a cigarette and gently blew the first exhalation above her head. 'And work—work—work—. We will start now with these Bach Inventions and these little Schumann pieces.' His hands moved again— this time to jerk the cord of the lamp behind her and point to the music. 'I will show you how I wish this practiced. Listen carefully now.'

She had been at the piano for almost three hours and was very tired. His deep voice sounded as though it had been straying inside her for a long time. She wanted to reach out and touch his muscle-flexed finger that pointed out the phrases, wanted to feel the gleaming gold band ring and the strong hairy back of his hand.

She had lessons Tuesday after school and on Saturday afternoons. Often she stayed, when the Saturday lesson was finished, for dinner, and then spent the night and took the streetcar home the next morning. Mrs. Bilderbach liked her in her calm, almost dumb way. She was much different from her husband. She was quiet and fat and slow. When she wasn't in the kitchen, cooking the rich dishes that both of them loved, she seemed to spend all her time in their bed upstairs, reading magazines or just looking with a half-smile at nothing. When they had married in Germany she had been a *lieder* singer. She didn't sing anymore (she said it was her throat). When he would call her in from the kitchen to listen to a pupil she would always smile and say that it was *gut,* very *gut.*

When Frances was thirteen it came to her one day that

the Bilderbachs had no children. It seemed strange. Once she had been back in the kitchen with Mrs. Bilderbach when he had come striding in from the studio, tense with anger at some pupil who had annoyed him. His wife stood stirring the thick soup until his hand groped out and rested on her shoulder. Then she turned—stood placid—while he folded his arms about her and buried his sharp face in the white, nerveless flesh of her neck. They stood that way without moving. And then his face jerked back suddenly, the anger diminished to a quiet inexpressiveness, and he had returned to the studio.

After she had started with Mister Bilderbach and didn't have time to see anything of the people at high school, Heime had been the only friend of her own age. He was Mister Lafkowitz's pupil and would come with him to Mister Bilderbach's on evenings when she would be there. They would listen to their teachers' playing. And often they themselves went over chamber music together—Mozart sonatas or Bloch.

A *Wunderkind*—a *Wunderkind*.

Heime was a *Wunderkind*. He and she, then.

Heime had been playing the violin since he was four. He didn't have to go to school; Mister Lafkowitz's brother, who was crippled, used to teach him geometry and European history and French verbs in the afternoon. When he was thirteen he had as fine a technique as any violinist in Cincinnati—everyone said so. But playing the violin must be easier than the piano. She knew it must be.

Heime always seemed to smell of corduroy pants and the food he had eaten and rosin. Half the time, too, his hands were dirty around the knuckles and the cuffs of his shirts peeped out dingily from the sleeves of his sweater. She always watched his hands when he played—thin only at the joints with the hard little blobs of flesh bulging over the short-cut nails and the babyish-looking crease that showed so plainly in his bowing wrist.

In the dreams, as when she was awake, she could remember the concert only in a blur. She had not known

81

it was unsuccessful for her until months after. True, the papers had praised Heime more than her. But he was much shorter than she. When they stood together on the stage he came only to her shoulders. And that made a difference with people, she knew. Also, there was the matter of the sonata they played together. The Bloch.

'No, no—I don't think that would be appropriate.' Mister Bilderbach had said when the Bloch was suggested to end the programme. 'Now that John Powell thing—the Sonate Virginianesque.'

She hadn't understood then; she wanted it to be the Bloch as much as Mister Lafkowitz and Heime.

Mister Bilderbach had given in. Later, after the reviews had said she lacked the temperament for that type of music, after they called her playing thin and lacking in feeling, she felt cheated.

'That oie oie stuff,' said Mister Bilderbach, crackling the newspapers at her. 'Not for you, Bienchen. Leave all that to the Heimes and vitses and skys.'

A *Wunderkind*. No matter what the papers said, that was what he had called her.

Why was it Heime had done so much better at the concert than she? At school sometimes, when she was supposed to be watching someone do a geometry problem on the blackboard, the question would twist knife-like inside her. She would worry about it in bed, and even sometimes when she was supposed to be concentrating at the piano. It wasn't just the Bloch and her not being Jewish—not entirely. It wasn't that Heime didn't have to go to school and had begun his training so early, either. It was——?

Once she thought she knew.

'Play the Fantasia and Fugue,' Mister Bilderbach had demanded one evening a year ago—after he and Mister Lafkowitz had finished reading some music together.

The Bach, as she played, seemed to her well done. From the tail of her eye she could see the calm, pleased expression on Mister Bilderbach's face, see his hands rise climactically from the chair arms and then sink down loose and satisfied when the high points of the phrases had been passed successfully. She stood up from the piano when it was over, swallowing to loosen the bands that the music seemed to have drawn around her throat and chest. But—

'Frances—' Mister Lafkowitz had said then, suddenly, looking at her with his thin mouth curved and his eyes almost covered by their delicate lids. 'Do you know how many children Bach had?'

She turned to him, puzzled. 'A good many. Twenty some odd.'

'Well then—' The corners of his smile etched themselves gently in his pale face. 'He could not have been so cold—then.'

Mister Bilderbach was not pleased; his guttural effulgence of German words had *Kind* in it somewhere. Mister Lafkowitz raised his eyebrows. She had caught the point easily enough, but she felt no deception in keeping her face blank and immature because that was the way Mister Bilderbach wanted her to look.

Yet such things had nothing to do with it. Nothing very much, at least, for she would grow older. Mister Bilderbach understood that, and even Mister Lafkowitz had not meant just what he said.

In the dreams Mister Bilderbach's face loomed out and contracted in the center of the whirling circle. The lips urging softly, the veins in his temples insisting.

But sometimes, before she slept, there were such clear memories; as when she pulled a hole in the heel of her stocking down, so that her shoe would hide it. 'Bienchen, Bienchen!' And bringing Mrs. Bilderbach's work basket in and showing her how it should be darned and not gathered together in a lumpy heap.

And the time she graduated from Junior High.

'What you wear?' asked Mrs. Bilderbach the Sunday morning at breakfast when she told them about how they had practiced to march into the auditorium.

'An evening dress my cousin had last year.'

'Ah—Bienchen!' he said, circling his warm coffee cup with his heavy hands, looking up at her with wrinkles around his laughing eyes. 'I bet I know what Bienchen wants—'

He insisted. He would not believe her when she explained that she honestly didn't care at all.

'Like this, Anna,' he said, pushing his napkin across the table and mincing to the other side of the room, swishing his hips, rolling up his eyes behind his horn-rimmed glasses.

The next Saturday afternoon, after her lessons, he took her to the department stores downtown. His thick fingers smoothed over the filmy nets and crackling taffetas that the saleswomen unwound from their bolts. He held colors to her face, cocking his head to one side, and selected pink. Shoes, he remembered too. He liked best some white kid pumps. They seemed a little like old ladies' shoes to her and the Red Cross label in the instep had a charity look. But it really didn't matter at all. When Mrs. Bilderbach began to cut out the dress and fit it to her with pins, he interrupted his lessons to stand by and suggest ruffles around the hips and neck and a fancy rosette on the shoulder. The music was coming along nicely then. Dresses and commencement and such made no difference.

Nothing mattered much except playing the music as it must be played, bringing out the thing that must be in her, practicing, practicing, playing so that Mister Bilderbach's face lost some of its urging look. Putting the thing into her music that Myra Hess had, and Yehudi Menuhin—even Heime!

What had begun to happen to her four months ago? The notes began springing out with a glib, dead intonation. Adolescence, she thought. Some kids played with promise—and worked and worked until, like her, the least little thing would start them crying, and worn out with trying to get the thing across—the longing thing they felt—something queer began to happen—But not she! She was like Heime. She had to be. She——

Once it was there for sure. And you didn't lose things like that. A *Wunderkind*. . . . A *Wunderkind*. . . . Of her he said it, rolling the words in the sure, deep German way. And in the dreams even deeper, more certain than ever. With his face looming out at her, and the longing phrases of music mixed in with the zooming, circling round, round, round—A *Wunderkind*. A *Wunderkind*. . . .

This afternoon Mister Bilderbach did not show Mister Lafkowitz to the front door, as he usually did. He stayed at the piano, softly pressing a solitary note. Listening, Frances watches the violinist wind his scarf about his pale throat.

'A good picture of Heime,' she said, picking up her music. 'I got a letter from him a couple of months ago— telling about hearing Schnabel and Huberman and about Carnegie Hall and things to eat at the Russian Tea Room.'

To put off going into the studio a moment longer she waited until Mister Lafkowitz was ready to leave and then stood behind him as he opened the door. The frosty cold outside cut into the room. It was growing late and the air was seeped with the pale yellow of winter twilight. When the door swung to on its hinges, the house seemed darker and more silent than ever before she had known it to be.

As she went into the studio Mister Bilderbach got up from the piano and silently watched her settle herself at the keyboard.

'Well, Bienchen,' he said, 'this afternoon we are going to begin all over. Start from scratch. Forget the last few months.'

He looked as though he were trying to act a part in a movie. His solid body swayed from toe to heel, he rubbed his hands together, and even smiled in a satisfied, movie way. Then suddenly he thrust this manner brusquely aside. His heavy shoulders slouched and he began to run through the stack of music she had brought in. 'The Bach—no, not yet,' he murmured. 'The Beethoven? Yes, the Variation Sonata. Opus. 26.'

The keys of the piano hemmed her in—stiff and white and dead-seeming.

'Wait a minute,' he said. He stood in the curve of the piano, elbows propped, and looked at her. 'Today I expect something from you. Now this sonata—it's the first Beethoven sonata you ever worked on. Every note is under control—technically—you have nothing to cope with but the music. Only music now. That's all you think about.'

He rustled through the pages of her volume until he found the place. Then he pulled his teaching chair half-way across the room, turned it around and seated himself, straddling the back with his legs.

For some reason, she knew, this position of his usually had a good effect on her performance. But today she felt that she would notice him from the corner of her eye and be disturbed. His back was stiffly tilted, his legs looked tense. The heavy volume before him seemed to balance dangerously on the chair back. 'Now we begin,' he said with a peremptory dart of his eyes in her direction.

Her hands rounded over the keys and then sank down. The first notes were too loud, the other phrases followed dryly.

Arrestingly his hand rose up from the score. 'Wait! Think a minute what you're playing. How is this beginning marked?'

'*An-andante.*'

'All right. Don't drag it into an *adagio* then. And play deeply into the keys. Don't snatch it off shallowly that way. A graceful, deep-toned *andante*—'

She tried again. Her hands seemed separate from the music that was in her.

'Listen,' he interrupted. 'Which of these variations dominates the whole?'

'The dirge,' she answered.

'Then prepare for that. This is an *andante*—but it's not salon stuff as you just played it. Start out softly, *piano,* and make it swell out just before the arpeggio.

86

Make it warm and dramatic. And down here—where it's marked *dolce* make the counter melody sing out. You know all that. We've gone over all that side of it before. Now play it. Feel it as Beethoven wrote it down. Feel that tragedy and restraint.'

She could not stop looking at his hands. They seemed to rest tentatively on the music, ready to fly up as a stop signal as soon as she would begin, the gleaming flash of his ring calling her to halt. 'Mister Bilderbach—maybe if I—if you let me play on through the first variation without stopping I could do better.'

'I won't interrupt,' he said.

Her pale face leaned over too close to the keys. She played through the first part, and, obeying a nod from him, began the second. There were no flaws that jarred on her, but the phrases shaped from her fingers before she had put into them the meaning that she felt.

When she had finished he looked up from the music and began to speak with dull bluntness: 'I hardly heard those harmonic fillings in the right hand. And incidentally, this part was supposed to take on intensity, develop the foreshadowings that were supposed to be inherent in the first part. Go on with the next one, though.'

She wanted to start it with subdued viciousness and progress to a feeling of deep, swollen sorrow. Her mind told her that. But her hands seemed to gum in the keys like limp macaroni and she could not imagine the music as it should be.

When the last note had stopped vibrating, he closed the book and deliberately got up from the chair. He was moving his lower jaw from side to side—and between his open lips she could glimpse the pink healthy lane to his throat and his strong, smoke-yellowed teeth. He laid the Beethoven gingerly on top of the rest of her music and propped his elbows on the smooth, black piano top once more. 'No,' he said simply, looking at her.

Her mouth began to quiver. 'I can't help it. I——'

Suddenly he strained his lips into a smile. 'Listen, Bienchen,' he began in a new, forced voice. 'You still

87

play the Harmonious Blacksmith, don't you? I told you not to drop it from your repertoire."

'Yes,' she said. 'I practice it now and then.'

His voice was the one he used for children. 'It was among the first things we worked on together—remember. So strongly you used to play it—like a real blacksmith's daughter. You see, Bienchen, I know you so well—as if you were my own girl. I know what you have—I've heard you play so many things beautifully. You used to——'

He stopped in confusion and inhaled from his pulpy stub of cigarette. The smoke drowsed out from his pink lips and clung in a gray mist around her lank hair and childish forehead.

'Make it happy and simple,' he said, switching on the lamp behind her and stepping back from the piano.

For a moment he stood just inside the bright circle the light made. Then impulsively he squatted down to the floor. 'Vigorous,' he said.

She could not stop looking at him, sitting on one heel with the other foot resting squarely before him for balance, the muscles of his strong thighs straining under the cloth of his trousers, his back straight, his elbows staunchly propped on his knees. 'Simply now,' he repeated with a gesture of his fleshy hands. 'Think of the blacksmith—working out in the sunshine all day. Working easily and undisturbed.'

She could not look down at the piano. The light brightened the hairs on the backs of his outspread hands, made the lenses of his glasses glitter.

'All of it,' he urged. 'Now!'

She felt that the marrows of her bones were hollow and there was no blood left in her. Her heart that had been springing against her chest all afternoon felt suddenly dead. She saw it gray and limp and shriveled at the edges like an oyster.

His face seemed to throb out in space before her, come closer with the lurching motion in the veins of his temples. In retreat, she looked down at the piano. Her lips shook like jelly and a surge of noiseless tears made the white keys blur in a watery line. 'I can't,' she whispered. 'I don't know why, but I just can't—can't any more.'

His tense body slackened and, holding his hand to his side, he pulled himself up. She clutched her music and hurried past him.

Her coat. The mittens and galoshes. The schoolbooks and the satchel he had given her on her birthday. All from the silent room that was hers. Quickly—before he would have to speak.

As she passed through the vestibule she could not help but see his hands—held out from his body that leaned against the studio door, relaxed and purposeless. The door shut to firmly. Dragging her books and satchel she stumbled down the stone steps, turned in the wrong direction, and hurried down the street that had become confused with noise and bicycles and the games of other children.

The Jockey

The Jockey

THE JOCKEY came to the doorway of the dining room, then after a moment stepped to one side and stood motionless, with his back to the wall. The room was crowded, as this was the third day of the season and all the hotels in the town were full. In the dining room bouquets of August roses scattered their petals on the white table linen and from the adjoining bar came a warm, drunken wash of voices. The jockey waited with his back to the wall and scrutinized the room with pinched, crêpy eyes. He examined the room until at last his eyes reached a table in a corner diagonally across from him, at which three men were sitting. As he watched, the jockey raised his chin and tilted his head back to one side, his dwarfed body grew rigid, and his hands stiffened so that the fingers curled inward like gray claws. Tense against the wall of the dining room, he watched and waited in this way.

He was wearing a suit of green Chinese silk that evening, tailored precisely and the size of a costume outfit for a child. The shirt was yellow, the tie striped with pastel colors. He had no hat with him and wore his hair brushed down in a stiff, wet bang on his forehead. His face was drawn, ageless, and gray. There were shadowed hollows at his temples and his mouth was set in a wiry smile. After a time he was aware that he had been seen by one of the three men he had been watching. But the jockey did not nod; he only raised his chin still higher and hooked the thumb of his tense hand in the pocket of his coat.

The three men at the corner table were a trainer, a bookie, and a rich man. The trainer was Sylvester—a large, loosely built fellow with a flushed nose and slow blue eyes. The bookie was Simmons. The rich man was the owner of a horse named Seltzer, which the jockey had ridden that afternoon. The three of them drank whiskey with soda, and a white-coated waiter had just brought on the main course of the dinner.

It was Sylvester who first saw the jockey. He looked away quickly, put down his whiskey glass, and nervously mashed the tip of his red nose with his thumb. 'It's Bitsy Barlow,' he said. 'Standing over there across the room. Just watching us.'

'Oh, the jockey,' said the rich man. He was facing the wall and he half turned his head to look behind him. 'Ask him over.'

'God no,' Sylvester said.

'He's crazy,' Simmons said. The bookie's voice was flat and without inflection. He had the face of a born gambler, carefully adjusted, the expression a permanent deadlock between fear and greed.

'Well, I wouldn't call him that exactly,' said Sylvester. 'I've known him a long time. He was O.K. until about six months ago. But if he goes on like this, I can't see him lasting another year. I just can't.'

'It was what happened in Miami,' said Simmons.

'What?' asked the rich man.

Sylvester glanced across the room at the jockey and wet the corner of his mouth with his red, fleshy tongue. 'A accident. A kid got hurt on the track. Broke a leg and a hip. He was a particular pal of Bitsy's. A Irish kid. Not a bad rider, either.'

'That's a pity,' said the rich man.

'Yeah. They were particular friends,' Sylvester said. 'You would always find him up in Bitsy's hotel room. They would be playing rummy or else lying on the floor reading the sports page together.'

'Well, those things happen,' said the rich man.

Simmons cut into his beefsteak. He held his fork

prongs downward on the plate and carefully piled on mushrooms with the blade of his knife. 'He's crazy,' he repeated. 'He gives me the creeps.'

All the tables in the dining room were occupied. There was a party at the banquet table in the center, and green-white August moths had found their way in from the night and fluttered about the clear candle flames. Two girls wearing flannel slacks and blazers walked arm in arm across the room into the bar. From the main street outside came the echoes of holiday hysteria.

'They claim that in August Saratoga is the wealthiest town per capita in the world.' Sylvester turned to the rich man. 'What do you think?'

'I wouldn't know,' said the rich man. 'It may very well be so.'

Daintily, Simmons wiped his greasy mouth with the tip of his forefinger. 'How about Hollywood? And Wall Street——'

'Wait,' said Sylvester. 'He's decided to come over here.'

The jockey had left the wall and was approaching the table in the corner. He walked with a prim strut, swinging out his legs in a half-circle with each step, his heels biting smartly into the red velvet carpet on the floor. On the way over he brushed against the elbow of a fat woman in white satin at the banquet table; he stepped back and bowed with dandified courtesy, his eyes quite closed. When he had crossed the room he drew up a chair and sat at a corner of the table, between Sylvester and the rich man, without a nod of greeting or a change in his set, gray face.

'Had dinner?' Sylvester asked.

'Some people might call it that.' The jockey's voice was high, bitter, clear.

Sylvester put his knife and fork down carefully on his plate. The rich man shifted his position, turning sidewise in his chair and crossing his legs. He was dressed in twill riding pants, unpolished boots, and a shabby brown jacket—this was his outfit day and night in the racing season, although he was never seen on a horse. Simmons went on with his dinner.

'Like a spot of seltzer water?' asked Sylvester. 'Or something like that?'

The jockey didn't answer. He drew a gold cigarette case from his pocket and snapped it open. Inside were a few cigarettes and a tiny gold penknife. He used the knife to cut a cigarette in half. When he had lighted his smoke he held up his hand to a waiter passing by the table. 'Kentucky bourbon, please.'

'Now, listen, Kid,' said Sylvester.

'Don't Kid me.'

'Be reasonable. You know you got to behave reasonable.'

The jockey drew up the left corner of his mouth in a stiff jeer. His eyes lowered to the food spread out on the table, but instantly he looked up again. Before the rich man was a fish casserole, baked in a cream sauce and garnished with parsley. Sylvester had ordered eggs Benedict. There was asparagus, fresh buttered corn, and a side dish of wet black olives. A plate of French-fried potatoes was in the corner of the table before the jockey. He didn't look at the food again, but kept his pinched eyes on the center piece of full-blown lavender roses. 'I don't suppose you remember a certain person by the name of McGuire,' he said.

'Now, listen,' said Sylvester.

The waiter brought the whiskey, and the jockey sat fondling the glass with his small, strong, callused hands. On his wrist was a gold link bracelet that clinked against the table edge. After turning the glass between his palms, the jockey suddenly drank the whiskey neat in two hard swallows. He set down the glass sharply. 'No, I don't suppose your memory is that long and extensive,' he said.

'Sure enough, Bitsy,' said Sylvester. 'What makes you act like this? You hear from the kid today?'

'I received a letter,' the jockey said. 'The certain person we were speaking about was taken out from the

cast on Wednesday. One leg is two inches shorter than
the other one. That's all.'

Sylvester clucked his tongue and shook his head. 'I
realize how you feel.'

'Do you?' The jockey was looking at the dishes on
the table. His gaze passed from the fish casserole to the
corn, and finally fixed on the plate of fried potatoes. His
face tightened and quickly he looked up again. A rose
shattered and he picked up one of the petals, bruised
it between his thumb and forefinger, and put it in his
mouth.

'Well, those things happen,' said the rich man.

The trainer and the bookie had finished eating, but
there was food left on the serving dishes before their
plates. The rich man dipped his buttery fingers in his
water glass and wiped them with his napkin.

'Well,' said the jockey. 'Doesn't somebody want me
to pass them something? Or maybe perhaps you desire
to re-order. Another hunk of beefsteak, gentlemen, or——'

'Please,' said Sylvester. 'Be reasonable. Why don't
you go on upstairs?'

'Yes, why don't I?' the jockey said.

His prim voice had risen higher and there was about
it the sharp whine of hysteria.

'Why don't I go up to my god-damn room and walk
around and write some letters and go to bed like a good
boy? Why don't I just——' He pushed his chair back and
got up. 'Oh, foo,' he said. 'Foo to you. I want a drink.'

'All I can say is it's your funeral,' said Sylvester.
'You know what it does to you. You know well enough.'

The jockey crossed the dining room and went into
the bar. He ordered a Manhattan, and Sylvester watched
him stand with his heels pressed tight together, his body
hard as a lead soldier's, holding his little finger out from
the cocktail glass and sipping the drink slowly.

'He's crazy,' said Simmons. 'Like I said.'

Sylvester turned to the rich man. 'If he eats a lamb
chop, you can see the shape of it in his stomach a hour
afterward. He can't sweat things out of him any more.

97

He's a hundred and twelve and a half. He's gained three pounds since we left Miami.'

'A jockey shouldn't drink,' said the rich man.

'The food don't satisfy him like it used to and he can't sweat it out. If he eats a lamb chop, you can watch it tooching out in his stomach and it don't go down.'

The jockey finished his Manhattan. He swallowed, crushed the cherry in the bottom of the glass with his thumb, then pushed the glass away from him. The two girls in blazers were standing at his left, their faces turned toward each other, and at the other end of the bar two touts had started an argument about which was the highest mountain in the world. Everyone was with somebody else; there was no other person drinking alone that night. The jockey paid with a brand-new fifty-dollar bill and didn't count the change.

He walked back to the dining room and to the table at which the three men were sitting, but he did not sit down. 'No, I wouldn't presume to think your memory is that extensive,' he said. He was so small that the edge of the table top reached almost to his belt, and when he gripped the corner with his wiry hands he didn't have to stoop. 'No, you're too busy gobbling up dinners in dining rooms. You're too——'

'Honestly,' begged Sylvester. 'You got to behave reasonable.'

'Reasonable! Reasonable!' The jockey's gray face quivered, then set in a mean, frozen grin. He shook the table so that the plates rattled, and for a moment it seemed that he would push it over. But suddenly he stopped. His hand reached out toward the plate nearest to him and deliberately he put a few of the French-fried potatoes in his mouth. He chewed slowly, his upper lip raised, then he turned and spat out the pulpy mouthful on the smooth red carpet which covered the floor. 'Libertines,' he said, and his voice was thin and broken. He rolled the word in his mouth, as though it had a flavor and a substance that gratified him. 'You libertines,' he said again, and turned and walked with his rigid swagger out of the dining room.

Sylvester shrugged one of his loose, heavy shoulders. The rich man sopped up some water that had been spilled on the tablecloth, and they didn't speak until the waiter came to clear away.

Madame Zilensky and
the King of Finland

Madame Zilensky and the King of Finland

To Mr. Brook, the head of the music department at Ryder College, was due all the credit for getting Madame Zilensky on the faculty. The college considered itself fortunate; her reputation was impressive, both as a composer and as a pedagogue. Mr. Brook took on himself the responsibility of finding a house for Madame Zilensky, a comfortable place with a garden, which was convenient to the college and next to the apartment house where he himself lived.

No one in Westbridge had known Madame Zilensky before she came. Mr. Brook had seen her pictures in musical journals, and once he had written to her about the authenticity of a certain Buxtehude manuscript. Also, when it was being settled that she was to join the faculty, they had exchanged a few cables and letters on practical affairs. She wrote in a clear, square hand, and the only thing out of the ordinary in these letters was the fact that they contained an occasional reference to objects and persons altogether unknown to Mr. Brook, such as 'the yellow cat in Lisbon' or 'poor Heinrich.' These lapses Mr. Brook put down to the confusion of getting herself and her family out of Europe.

Mr. Brook was a somewhat pastel person; years of Mozart minuets, of explanations about diminished sevenths and minor triads, had given him a watchful vocational patience. For the most part, he kept to himself. He loathed academic fiddle-faddle and committees. Years before, when the music department had decided to gang together and spend the summer in Salzburg, Mr. Brook sneaked out of the arrangement at the last moment and took a solitary trip to Peru. He had a few eccentricities himself and was tolerant of the peculiarities of others; indeed, he rather relished the ridiculous. Often, when confronted with some grave and incongruous situation, he would feel a little inside tickle, which stiffened his long, mild face and sharpened the light in his gray eyes.

Mr. Brook met Madame Zilensky at the Westbridge station a week before the beginning of the fall semester. He recognized her instantly. She was a tall, straight woman with a pale and haggard face. Her eyes were deeply shadowed and she wore her dark, ragged hair pushed back from her forehead. She had large, delicate hands, which were very grubby. About her person as a whole there was something noble and abstract that made Mr. Brook draw back for a moment and stand nervously undoing his cuff links. In spite of her clothes—a long, black skirt and a broken-down old leather jacket—she made an impression of vague elegance. With Madame Zilensky were three children, boys between the ages of ten and six, all blond, blank-eyed, and beautiful. There was one other person, an old woman who turned out later to be the Finnish servant.

This was the group he found at the station. The only luggage they had with them was two immense boxes of manuscripts, the rest of their paraphernalia having been forgotten in the station at Springfield when they changed trains. That is the sort of thing that can happen to anyone. When Mr. Brook got them all into a taxi, he thought the worst difficulties were over, but Madame Zilensky suddenly tried to scramble over his knees and get out of the door.

'My God!' she said. 'I left my—how do you say?—my tick-tick-tick——'

'Your watch?' asked Mr. Brook.

'Oh no!' she said vehemently. 'You know, my tick-tick-tick,' and she waved her forefinger from side to side, pendulum fashion.

'Tick-tick,' said Mr. Brook, putting his hands to his

forehead and closing his eyes. 'Could you possibly mean a metronome?'

'Yes! Yes! I think I must have lost it there where we changed trains.'

Mr. Brook managed to quiet her. He even said, with a kind of dazed gallantry, that he would get her another one the next day. But at the time he was bound to admit to himself that there was something curious about this panic over a metronome when there was all the rest of the lost luggage to consider.

The Zilensky ménage moved into the house next door, and on the surface everything was all right. The boys were quiet children. Their names were Sigmund, Boris, and Sammy. They were always together and they followed each other around Indian file, Sigmund usually the first. Among themselves they spoke a desperate-sounding family Esperanto made up of Russian, French, Finnish, German, and English; when other people were around, they were strangely silent. It was not any one thing that the Zilenskys did or said that made Mr. Brook uneasy. There were just little incidents. For example, something about the Zilensky children subconsciously bothered him when they were in a house, and finally he realized that what troubled him was the fact that the Zilensky boys never walked on a rug; they skirted it single file on the bare floor, and if a room was carpeted, they stood in the doorway and did not go inside. Another thing was this: Weeks passed and Madame Zilensky seemed to make no effort to get settled or to furnish the house with anything more than a table and some beds. The front door was left open day and night, and soon the house began to take on a queer, bleak look like that of a place abandoned for years.

The college had every reason to be satisfied with Madame Zilensky. She taught with a fierce insistence. She could become deeply indignant if some Mary Owens or Bernadine Smith would not clean up her Scarlatti trills. She got hold of four pianos for her college studio and set four dazed students to playing Bach fugues together. The racket that came from her end of the department was extraordinary, but Madame Zilensky did not seem to have a nerve in her, and if pure will and effort can get over a musical idea, then Ryder College could not have done better. At night Madame Zilensky worked on her twelfth symphony. She seemed never to sleep; no matter what time of night Mr. Brook happened to look out of his sitting-room window, the light in her studio was always on. No, it was not because of any professional consideration that Mr. Brook became so dubious.

It was in late October when he felt for the first time that something was unmistakably wrong. He had lunched with Madame Zilensky and had enjoyed himself, as she had given him a very detailed account of an African safari she had made in 1928. Later in the afternoon she stopped in at his office and stood rather abstractly in the doorway.

Mr. Brook looked up from his desk and asked, 'Is there anything you want?'

'No, thank you,' said Madame Zilensky. She had a low, beautiful, sombre voice. 'I was only just wondering. You recall the metronome. Do you think perhaps that I might have left it with that French?'

'Who?' asked Mr. Brook.

'Why, that French I was married to,' she answered.

'Frenchman,' Mr. Brook said mildly. He tried to imagine the husband of Madame Zilensky, but his mind refused. He muttered half to himself, 'The father of the children.'

'But no,' said Madame Zilensky with decision. 'The father of Sammy.'

Mr. Brook had a swift prescience. His deepest instincts warned him to say nothing further. Still, his respect for order, his conscience, demanded that he ask, 'And the father of the other two?'

Madame Zilensky put her hand to the back of her head and ruffled up her short, cropped hair. Her face was dreamy, and for several moments she did not answer. Then she said gently, 'Boris is of a Pole who played the piccolo.'

'And Sigmund?' he asked. Mr. Brook looked over his orderly desk, with the stack of corrected papers, the three sharpened pencils, the ivory-elephant paperweight. When he glanced up at Madame Zilensky, she was obviously thinking hard. She gazed around at the corners of the room, her brows lowered and her jaw moving from side to side. At last she said, 'We were discussing the father of Sigmund?'

'Why, no,' said Mr. Brook. 'There is no need to do that.'

Madame Zilensky answered in a voice both dignified and final. 'He was a fellow-countryman.'

Mr. Brook really did not care one way or the other. He had no prejudices; people could marry seventeen times and have Chinese children so far as he was concerned. But there was something about this conversation with Madame Zilensky that bothered him. Suddenly he understood. The children didn't look at all like Madame Zilensky, but they looked exactly like each other, and as they all had different fathers, Mr. Brook thought the resemblance astonishing.

But Madame Zilensky had finished with the subject. She zipped up her leather jacket and turned away.

'That is exactly where I left it,' she said, with a quick nod. '*Chez* that French.'

Affairs in the music department were running smoothly. Mr. Brook did not have any serious embarrassments to deal with, such as the harp teacher last year who had finally eloped with a garage mechanic. There was only this nagging apprehension about Madame Zilensky. He could not make out what was wrong in his relations with her or why his feelings were so mixed. To begin with, she was a great globe-trotter, and her conversations were incongruously seasoned with references to far-fetched places. She would go along for days without opening her mouth, prowling through the corridor with her hands in the pockets of her jacket and her face locked in meditation. Then suddenly she would buttonhole Mr. Brook and launch out on a long, volatile monologue, her eyes reckless and bright and her voice warm with eagerness. She would talk about anything or nothing at all. Yet, without exception, there was something queer, in a slanted sort of way, about every episode she ever mentioned. If she spoke of taking Sammy to the barbershop, the impression she created was just as foreign as if she were telling of an afternoon in Bagdad. Mr. Brook could not make it out.

The truth came to him very suddenly, and the truth made everything perfectly clear, or at least clarified the situation. Mr. Brook had come home early and lighted a fire in the little grate in his sitting room. He felt comfortable and at peace that evening. He sat before the fire in his stocking feet, with a volume of William Blake on the table by his side, and he had poured himself a half-glass of apricot brandy. At ten o'clock he was drowsing cozily before the fire, his mind full of cloudy phrases of Mahler and floating half-thoughts. Then all at once, out of this delicate stupor, four words came to his mind: 'The King of Finland.' The words seemed familiar, but for the first moment he could not place them. Then all at once he tracked them down. He had been walking across the campus that afternoon when Madame Zilensky stopped him and began some preposterous rigamarole, to which he had only half listened; he was thinking about the stack of canons turned in by his counterpoint class. Now the words, the inflections of her voice, came back to him with insidious exactitude. Madame Zilensky had started off with the following remark: 'One day, when I was standing in front of a *pâtisserie*, the King of Finland came by in a sled.'

Mr. Brook jerked himself up straight in his chair and put down his glass of brandy. The woman was a pathological liar. Almost every word she uttered outside of class was an untruth. If she worked all night, she would go out of her way to tell you she spent the evening at the cinema. If she ate lunch at the Old Tavern, she would be sure to mention that she had lunched with her children at home. The woman was simply a pathological liar, and that accounted for everything.

Mr. Brook cracked his knuckles and got up from his chair. His first reaction was one of exasperation. That day after day Madame Zilensky would have the gall to sit there in his office and deluge him with her outrageous falsehoods! Mr. Brook was intensely provoked. He walked up and down the room, then he went into his kitchenette and made himself a sardine sandwich.

An hour later, as he sat before the fire, his irritation had changed to a scholarly and thoughtful wonder. What he must do, he told himself, was to regard the whole situation impersonally and look on Madame Zilensky as a doctor looks on a sick patient. Her lies were of the guileless sort. She did not dissimulate with any intention to deceive, and the untruths she told were never used to any possible advantage. That was the maddening thing; there was simply no motive behind it all.

Mr. Brook finished off the rest of the brandy. And slowly, when it was almost midnight, a further understanding came to him. The reason for the lies of Madame Zilensky was painful and plain. All her life long Madame Zilensky had worked—at the piano, teaching, and writing those beautiful and immense twelve symphonies. Day and night she had drudged and struggled and thrown her soul into her work, and there was not much of her left over for anything else. Being human, she suffered from this lack and did what she could to make up for it. If she passed the evening bent over a table in the library and later declared that she had spent that time playing cards, it was as though she had managed to do both those things. Through the lies, she lived vicariously. The lies doubled the little of her existence that was left over from work and augmented the little rag end of her personal life.

Mr. Brook looked into the fire, and the face of Madame Zilensky was in his mind—a severe face, with dark, weary eyes and delicately disciplined mouth. He was conscious of a warmth in his chest, and a feeling of pity, protectiveness, and dreadful understanding. For a while he was in a state of lovely confusion.

Later on he brushed his teeth and got into his pajamas. He must be practical. What did this clear up? That French, the Pole with the piccolo, Bagdad? And the children, Sigmund, Boris, and Sammy—who were they? Were they really her children after all, or had she simply rounded them up from somewhere? Mr. Brook polished his spectacles and put them on the table by his bed. He must come to an immediate understanding with her. Otherwise, there would exist in the department a situation which could become most problematical. It was two o'clock. He glanced out of his window and saw that the light in Madame Zilensky's workroom was still on. Mr. Brook got into bed, made terrible faces in the dark, and tried to plan what he would say next day.

Mr. Brook was in his office by eight o'clock. He sat hunched up behind his desk, ready to trap Madame Zilensky as she passed down the corridor. He did not have to wait long, and as soon as he heard her footsteps he called out her name.

Madame Zilensky stood in the doorway. She looked vague and jaded. 'How are you? I had such a fine night's rest,' she said.

'Pray be seated, if you please,' said Mr. Brook. 'I would like a word with you.'

Madame Zilensky put aside her portfolio and leaned back wearily in the armchair across from him. 'Yes?' she asked.

'Yesterday you spoke to me as I was walking across the campus,' he said slowly. 'And if I am not mistaken, I believe you said something about a pastry shop and the King of Finland. Is that correct?'

Madame Zilensky turned her head to one side and stared retrospectively at a corner of the window sill.

'Something about a pastry shop,' he repeated.

Her tired face brightened. 'But of course,' she said eagerly. 'I told you about the time I was standing in front of this shop and the King of Finland——'

'Madame Zilensky!' Mr. Brook cried. 'There *is* no King of Finland.'

Madame Zilensky looked absolutely blank. Then, after an instant, she started off again. 'I was standing in front of Bjarne's *pâtisserie* when I turned away from the cakes and suddenly saw the King of Finland——'

'Madame Zilensky, I just told you that there is no King of Finland.'

'In Helsingfors,' she started off again desperately, and again he let her get as far as the King, and then no further.

'Finland is a democracy,' he said. 'You could not possibly have seen the King of Finland. Therefore, what you have just said is an untruth. A pure untruth.'

Never afterward could Mr. Brook forget the face of Madame Zilensky at that moment. In her eyes there was astonishment, dismay, and a sort of cornered horror. She had the look of one who watches his whole interior world split open and disintegrate.

'It is a pity,' said Mr. Brook with real sympathy.

But Madame Zilensky pulled herself together. She raised her chin and said coldly, 'I am a Finn.'

'That I do not question,' answered Mr. Brook. On second thought, he did question it a little.

'I was born in Finland and I am a Finnish citizen.'

'That may very well be,' said Mr. Brook in a rising voice.

'In the war,' she continued passionately, 'I rode a motorcycle and was a messenger.'

'Your patriotism does not enter into it.'

'Just because I am getting out the first papers——'

'Madame Zilensky!' said Mr. Brook. His hands grasped the edge of the desk. 'That is only an irrelevant issue. The point is that you maintained and testified that you saw—that you saw——' But he could not finish. Her face stopped him. She was deadly pale and there were shadows around her mouth. Her eyes were wide open, doomed, and proud. And Mr. Brook felt suddenly like a murderer. A great commotion of feelings—understanding, remorse, and unreasonable love—made him cover his face with his hands. He could not speak until this agitation in his insides quieted down, and then he said very faintly, 'Yes. Of course. The King of Finland. And was he nice?'

An hour later, Mr. Brook sat looking out of the window of his office. The trees along the quiet Westbridge street were almost bare, and the gray buildings of the college had a calm, sad look. As he idly took in the familiar scene, he noticed the Drakes' old Airedale waddling along down the street. It was a thing he had watched a hundred times before, so what was it that struck him as strange? Then he realized with a kind of cold surprise that the old dog was running along backward. Mr. Brook watched the Airedale until he was out of sight, then resumed his work on the canons which had been turned in by the class in counterpoint.

The Sojourner

The Sojourner

THE TWILIGHT BORDER between sleep and waking was a Roman one this morning; splashing fountains and arched, narrow streets, the golden lavish city of blossoms and age-soft stone. Sometimes in this semi-consciousness he sojourned again in Paris, or war German rubble, or Swiss skiing and a snow hotel. Sometimes, also, in a fallow Georgia field at hunting dawn. Rome it was this morning in the yearless region of dreams.

John Ferris awoke in a room in a New York hotel. He had the feeling that something unpleasant was awaiting him—what it was, he did not know. The feeling, submerged by matinal necessities, lingered even after he had dressed and gone downstairs. It was a cloudless autumn day and the pale sunlight sliced between the pastel skyscrapers. Ferris went into the next-door drugstore and sat at the end booth next to the window glass that overlooked the sidewalk. He ordered an American breakfast with scrambled eggs and sausage.

Ferris had come from Paris to his father's funeral which had taken place the week before in his home town in Georgia. The shock of death had made him aware of youth already passed. His hair was receding and the veins in his now naked temples were pulsing and prominent and his body was spare except for an incipient belly bulge. Ferris had loved his father and the bond between them had once been extraordinarily close—but the years had somehow unraveled this filial devotion; the death, expected for a long time, had left him with an unforeseen dismay. He had stayed as long

115

as possible to be near his mother and brothers at home. His plane for Paris was to leave the next morning.

Ferris pulled out his address book to verify a number. He turned the pages with growing attentiveness. Names and addresses from New York, the capitals of Europe, a few faint ones from his home state in the South. Faded, printed names, sprawled drunken ones. Betty Wills: a random love, married now. Charlie Williams: wounded in the Hürtgen Forest, unheard of since. Grand old Williams—did he live or die? Don Walker: a B.T.O. in television, getting rich. Henry Green: hit the skids after the war, in a sanitarium now, they say. Cozie Hall: he had heard that she was dead. Heedless, laughing Cozie— it was strange to think that she too, silly girl, could die. As Ferris closed the address book, he suffered a sense of hazard, transience, almost of fear.

It was then that his body jerked suddenly. He was staring out of the window when there, on the sidewalk, passing by, was his ex-wife. Elizabeth passed quite close to him, walking slowly. He could not understand the wild quiver of his heart, nor the following sense of recklessness and grace that lingered after she was gone.

Quickly Ferris paid his check and rushed out to the sidewalk. Elizabeth stood on the corner waiting to cross Fifth Avenue. He hurried toward her meaning to speak, but the lights changed and she crossed the street before he reached her. Ferris followed. On the other side he could easily have overtaken her, but he found himself lagging unaccountably. Her fair brown hair was plainly rolled, and as he watched her Ferris recalled that once his father had remarked that Elizabeth had a 'beautiful carriage.' She turned at the next corner and Ferris followed, although by now his intention to overtake her had disappeared. Ferris questioned the bodily disturbance that the sight of Elizabeth aroused in him, the dampness of his hands, the hard heart-strokes.

It was eight years since Ferris had last seen his ex-wife. He knew that long ago she had married again. And there were children. During recent years he had seldom thought of her. But at first, after the divorce, the loss had almost destroyed him. Then after the anodyne of time, he had loved again, and then again. Jeannine, she was now. Certainly his love for his ex-wife was long since past. So why the unhinged body, the shaken mind? He knew only that his clouded heart was oddly dissonant with the sunny, candid autumn day. Ferris wheeled suddenly and, walking with long strides, almost running, hurried back to the hotel.

Ferris poured himself a drink, although it was not yet eleven o'clock. He sprawled out in an armchair like a man exhausted, nursing his glass of bourbon and water. He had a full day ahead of him as he was leaving by plane the next morning for Paris. He checked over his obligations: take luggage to Air France, lunch with his boss, buy shoes and an overcoat. And something—wasn't there something else? Ferris finished his drink and opened the telephone directory.

His decision to call his ex-wife was impulsive. The number was under Bailey, the husband's name, and he called before he had much time for self-debate. He and Elizabeth had exchanged cards at Christmastime, and Ferris had sent a carving set when he received the announcement of her wedding. There was no reason *not* to call. But as he waited, listening to the ring at the other end, misgiving fretted him.

Elizabeth answered; her familiar voice was a fresh shock to him. Twice he had to repeat his name, but when he was identified, she sounded glad. He explained he was only in town for that day. They had a theater engagement, she said—but she wondered if he would come by for an early dinner. Ferris said he would be delighted.

As he went from one engagement to another, he was still bothered at odd moments by the feeling that something necessary was forgotten. Ferris bathed and changed in the late afternoon, often thinking about Jeannine: he would be with her the following night. 'Jeannine,' he would say, 'I happened to run into my ex-wife when

I was in New York. Had dinner with her. And her husband, of course. It was strange seeing her after all these years.'

Elizabeth lived in the East Fifties, and as Ferris taxied uptown he glimpsed at intersections the lingering sunset, but by the time he reached his destination it was already autumn dark. The place was a building with a marquee and a doorman, and the apartment was on the seventh floor.

'Come in, Mr. Ferris.'

Braced for Elizabeth or even the unimagined husband, Ferris was astonished by the freckled red-haired child; he had known of the children, but his mind had failed somehow to acknowledge them. Surprise made him step back awkwardly.

'This is our apartment,' the child said politely. 'Aren't you Mr. Ferris? I'm Billy. Come in.'

In the living room beyond the hall, the husband provided another surprise; he too had not been acknowledged emotionally. Bailey was a lumbering red-haired man with a deliberate manner. He rose and extended a welcoming hand.

'I'm Bill Bailey. Glad to see you. Elizabeth will be in, in a minute. She's finishing dressing.'

The last words struck a gliding series of vibrations, memories of the other years. Fair Elizabeth, rosy and naked before her bath. Half-dressed before the mirror of her dressing table, brushing her fine, chestnut hair. Sweet, casual intimacy, the soft-fleshed loveliness indisputably possessed. Ferris shrank from the unbidden memories and compelled himself to meet Bill Bailey's gaze.

'Billy, will you please bring that tray of drinks from the kitchen table?'

The child obeyed promptly, and when he was gone Ferris remarked conversationally, 'Fine boy you have there.'

'We think so.'

Flat silence until the child returned with a tray of

glasses and a cocktail shaker of Martinis. With the priming drinks they pumped up conversation: Russia, they spoke of, and the New York rain-making, and the apartment situation in Manhattan and Paris.

'Mr. Ferris is flying all the way across the ocean tomorrow,' Bailey said to the little boy who was perched on the arm of his chair, quiet and well behaved. 'I bet you would like to be a stowaway in his suitcase.'

Billy pushed back his limp bangs. 'I want to fly in an airplane and be a newspaperman like Mr. Ferris.' He added with sudden assurance, 'That's what I would like to do when I am big.'

Bailey said, 'I thought you wanted to be a doctor.'

'I do!' said Billy. 'I would like to be both. I want to be a atom-bomb scientist too.'

Elizabeth came in carrying in her arms a baby girl.

'Oh, John!' she said. She settled the baby in the father's lap. 'It's grand to see you. I'm awfully glad you could come.'

The little girl sat demurely on Bailey's knees. She wore a pale pink crêpe de Chine frock, smocked around the yoke with rose, and a matching silk hair ribbon tying back her pale soft curls. Her skin was summer tanned and her brown eyes flecked with gold and laughing. When she reached up and fingered her father's horn-rimmed glasses, he took them off and let her look through them a moment. 'How's my old Candy?'

Elizabeth was very beautiful, more beautiful perhaps than he had ever realized. Her straight clean hair was shining. Her face was softer, glowing and serene. It was a madonna loveliness, dependent on the family ambiance.

'You've hardly changed at all,' Elizabeth said, 'but it has been a long time.'

'Eight years.' His hand touched his thinning hair self-consciously while further amenities were exchanged.

Ferris felt himself suddenly a spectator—an interloper among these Baileys. Why had he come? He suffered. His own life seemed so solitary, a fragile column supporting nothing amidst the wreckage of the years. He felt he could not bear much longer to stay in the family room.

He glanced at his watch. 'You're going to the theater?'

'It's a shame,' Elizabeth said, 'but we've had this engagement for more than a month. But surely, John, you'll be staying home one of these days before long. You're not going to be an expatriate, are you?'

'Expatriate,' Ferris repeated. 'I don't much like the word.'

'What's a better word?' she asked.

He thought for a moment. 'Sojourner might do.'

Ferris glanced again at his watch, and again Elizabeth apologized. 'If only we had known ahead of time——'

'I just had this day in town. I came home unexpectedly. You see, Papa died last week.'

'Papa Ferris is dead?'

'Yes, at Johns-Hopkins. He had been sick there nearly a year. The funeral was down home in Georgia.'

'Oh, I'm so sorry, John. Papa Ferris was always one of my favorite people.'

The little boy moved from behind the chair so that he could look into his mother's face. He asked, 'Who is dead?'

Ferris was oblivious to apprehension; he was thinking of his father's death. He saw again the outstretched body on the quilted silk within the coffin. The corpse flesh was bizarrely rouged and the familiar hands lay massive and joined above a spread of funeral roses. The memory closed and Ferris awakened to Elizabeth's calm voice.

'Mr. Ferris' father, Billy. A really grand person. Somebody you didn't know.'

'But why did you call him *Papa* Ferris?'

Bailey and Elizabeth exchanged a trapped look. It was Bailey who answered the questioning child. 'A long time ago,' he said, 'your mother and Mr. Ferris were once married. Before you were born—a long time ago.'

'Mr. Ferris?'

The little boy stared at Ferris, amazed and unbelieving. And Ferris' eyes, as he returned the gaze, were somehow unbelieving too. Was it indeed true that at one time he had called this stranger, Elizabeth, Little Butterduck during nights of love, that they had lived together, shared perhaps a thousand days and nights and—finally—endured in the misery of sudden solitude the fiber by fiber (jealousy, alcohol and money quarrels) destruction of the fabric of married love.

Bailey said to the children, 'It's somebody's supper-time. Come on now.'

'But Daddy! Mama and Mr. Ferris—I——'

Billy's everlasting eyes—perplexed and with a glimmer of hostility—reminded Ferris of the gaze of another child. It was the young son of Jeannine—a boy of seven with a shadowed little face and knobby knees whom Ferris avoided and usually forgot.

'Quick march!' Bailey gently turned Billy toward the door. 'Say good night now, son.'

'Good night, Mr. Ferris.' He added resentfully, 'I thought I was staying up for the cake.'

'You can come in afterward for the cake,' Elizabeth said. 'Run along now with Daddy for your supper.'

Ferris and Elizabeth were alone. The weight of the situation descended on those first moments of silence. Ferris asked permission to pour himself another drink and Elizabeth set the cocktail shaker on the table at his side. He looked at the grand piano and noticed the music on the rack.

'Do you still play as beautifully as you used to?'

'I still enjoy it.'

'Please play, Elizabeth.'

Elizabeth arose immediately. Her readiness to perform when asked had always been one of her amiabilities; she never hung back, apologized. Now as she approached the piano there was the added readiness of relief.

She began with a Bach prelude and fugue. The prelude was as gaily iridescent as a prism in a morning room. The first voice of the fugue, an announcement pure and solitary, was repeated intermingling with a second voice, and again repeated within an elaborated frame, the multiple music, horizontal and serene, flowed with unhurried majesty. The principal melody was woven with two other voices, embellished with countless ingenuities—now dominant, again submerged, it had the sublimity of a single thing that does not fear surrender to the whole. Toward the end, the density of the material gathered for the last enriched insistence on the dominant first motif and with a chorded final statement the fugue ended. Ferris rested his head on the chair back and closed his eyes. In the following silence a clear, high voice came from the room down the hall.

'Daddy, how *could* Mama and Mr. Ferris——' A door was closed.

The piano began again—what was this music? Unplaced, familiar, the limpid melody had lain a long while dormant in his heart. Now it spoke to him of another time, another place—it was the music Elizabeth used to play. The delicate air summoned a wilderness of memory. Ferris was lost in the riot of past longings, conflicts, ambivalent desires. Strange that the music, catalyst for this tumultuous anarchy, was so serene and clear. The singing melody was broken off by the appearance of the maid.

'Miz Bailey, dinner is out on the table now.'

Even after Ferris was seated at the table between his host and hostess, the unfinished music still overcast his mood. He was a little drunk.

'*L'improvisation de la vie humaine,*' he said. 'There's nothing that makes you so aware of the improvisation of human existence as a song unfinished. Or an old address book.'

'Address book?' repeated Bailey. Then he stopped, noncommittal and polite.

'You're still the same old boy, Johnny,' Elizabeth said with a trace of the old tenderness.

It was a Southern dinner that evening, and the dishes were his old favorites. They had fried chicken and corn pudding and rich, glazed candied sweet potatoes. During the meal Elizabeth kept alive a conversation when the silences were overlong. And it came about that Ferris was led to speak of Jeannine.

'I first knew Jeannine last autumn—about this time of the year—in Italy. She's a singer and she had an engagement in Rome. I expect we will be married soon.'

The words seemed so true, inevitable, that Ferris did not at first acknowledge to himself the lie. He and Jeannine had never in that year spoken of marriage. And indeed, she was still married—to a White Russian moneychanger in Paris from whom she had been separated for five years. But it was too late to correct the lie. Already Elizabeth was saying: 'This really makes me glad to know. Congratulations, Johnny.'

He tried to make amends with truth. 'The Roman autumn is so beautiful. Balmy and blossoming.' He added, 'Jeannine has a little boy of six. A curious trilingual little fellow. We go to the Tuileries sometimes.'

A lie again. He had taken the boy once to the gardens. The sallow foreign child in shorts that bared his spindly legs had sailed his boat in the concrete pond and ridden the pony. The child had wanted to go in to the puppet show. But there was not time, for Ferris had an engagement at the Scribe Hotel. He had promised they would go to the guignol another afternoon. Only once had he taken Valentin to the Tuileries.

There was a stir. The maid brought in a white-frosted cake with pink candles. The children entered in their night clothes. Ferris still did not understand.

'Happy birthday, John,' Elizabeth said. 'Blow out the candles.'

Ferris recognized his birthday date. The candles blew out lingeringly and there was the smell of burning wax. Ferris was thirty-eight years old. The veins in his temples darkened and pulsed visibly.

'It's time you started for the theater.'

Ferris thanked Elizabeth for the birthday dinner and said the appropriate good-byes. The whole family saw him to the door.

A high, thin moon shone above the jagged, dark skyscrapers. The streets were windy, cold. Ferris hurried to Third Avenue and hailed a cab. He gazed at the nocturnal city with the deliberate attentiveness of departure and perhaps farewell. He was alone. He longed for flighttime and the coming journey.

The next day he looked down on the city from the air, burnished in sunlight, toylike, precise. Then America was left behind and there was only the Atlantic and the distant European shore. The ocean was milky pale and placid beneath the clouds. Ferris dozed most of the day. Toward dark he was thinking of Elizabeth and the visit of the previous evening. He thought of Elizabeth among her family with longing, gentle envy and inexplicable regret. He sought the melody, the unfinished air, that had so moved him. The cadence, some unrelated tones, were all that remained; the melody itself evaded him. He had found instead the first voice of the fugue that Elizabeth had played—it came to him, inverted mockingly and in a minor key. Suspended above the ocean the anxieties of transience and solitude no longer troubled him and he thought of his father's death with equanimity. During the dinner hour the plane reached the shore of France.

At midnight Ferris was in a taxi crossing Paris. It was a clouded night and mist wreathed the lights of the Place de la Concorde. The midnight bistros gleamed on the wet pavements. As always after a transocean flight the change of continents was too sudden. New York at morning, this midnight Paris. Ferris glimpsed the disorder of his life: the succession of cities, of transitory loves; and time, the sinister glissando of the years, time always.

'*Vite! Vite!*' he called in terror. '*Dépêchez-vous.*'

Valentin opened the door to him. The little boy wore pajamas and an outgrown red robe. His grey eyes were shadowed and, as Ferris passed into the flat, they flickered momentarily.

'*J'attends Maman.*'

Jeannine was singing in a night club. She would not

be home before another hour. Valentin returned to a drawing, squatting with his crayons over the paper on the floor. Ferris looked down at the drawing—it was a banjo player with notes and wavy lines inside a comic-strip balloon.

'We will go again to the Tuileries.'

The child looked up and Ferris drew him closer to his knees. The melody, the unfinished music that Elizabeth had played, came to him suddenly. Unsought, the load of memory jettisoned—this time bringing only recognition and sudden joy.

'Monsieur Jean,' the child said, 'did you see him?'

Confused, Ferris thought only of another child—the freckled, family-loved boy. 'See who, Valentin?'

'Your dead papa in Georgia.' The child added, 'Was he okay?'

Ferris spoke with rapid urgency: 'We will go often to the Tuileries. Ride the pony and we will go into the guignol. We will see the puppet show and never be in a hurry any more.'

'Monsieur Jean,' Valentin said. 'The guignol is now closed.'

Again, the terror the acknowledgment of wasted years and death. Valentin, responsive and confident, still nestled in his arms. His cheek touched the soft cheek and felt the brush of the delicate eyelashes. With inner desperation he pressed the child close—as though an emotion as protean as his love could dominate the pulse of time.

A Domestic Dilemma

A Domestic Dilemma

On Thursday Martin Meadows left the office early enough to make the first express bus home. It was the hour when the evening lilac glow was fading in the slushy streets, but by the time the bus had left the mid-town terminal the bright city night had come. On Thursdays the maid had a half-day off and Martin liked to get home as soon as possible, since for the past year his wife had not been—well. This Thursday he was very tired and, hoping that no regular commuter would single him out for conversation, he fastened his attention to the newspaper until the bus had crossed the George Washington Bridge. Once on 9-W Highway Martin always felt that the trip was halfway done, he breathed deeply, even in cold weather when only ribbons of draught cut through the smoky air of the bus, confident that he was breathing country air. It used to be that at this point he would relax and begin to think with pleasure of his home. But in this last year nearness brought only a sense of tension and he did not anticipate the journey's end. This evening Martin kept his face close to the window and watched the barren fields and lonely lights of passing townships. There was a moon, pale on the dark earth and areas of late, porous snow; to Martin the countryside seemed vast and somehow desolate that evening. He took his hat from the rack and put his folded newspaper in the pocket of his overcoat a few minutes before time to pull the cord.

The cottage was a block from the bus stop, near the river but not directly on the shore; from the living-room

129

window you could look across the street and opposite yard and see the Hudson. The cottage was modern, almost too white and new on the narrow plot of yard. In summer the grass was soft and bright and Martin carefully tended a flower border and a rose trellis. But during the cold, fallow months the yard was bleak and the cottage seemed naked. Lights were on that evening in all the rooms in the little house and Martin hurried up the front walk. Before the steps he stopped to move a wagon out of the way.

The children were in the living room, so intent on play that the opening of the front door was at first unnoticed. Martin stood looking at his safe, lovely children. They had opened the bottom drawer of the secretary and taken out the Christmas decorations. Andy had managed to plug in the Christmas tree lights and the green and red bulbs glowed with out-of-season festivity on the rug of the living room. At the moment he was trying to trail the bright cord over Marianne's rocking horse. Marianne sat on the floor pulling off an angel's wings. The children wailed a startling welcome. Martin swung the fat little baby girl up to his shoulder and Andy threw himself against his father's legs.

'Daddy, Daddy, Daddy!'

Martin set down the little girl carefully and swung Andy a few times like a pendulum. Then he picked up the Christmas tree cord.

'What's all this stuff doing out? Help me put it back in the drawer. You're not to fool with the light socket. Remember I told you that before. I mean it, Andy.'

The six-year-old child nodded and shut the secretary drawer. Martin stroked his fair soft hair and his hand lingered tenderly on the nape of the child's frail neck.

'Had supper yet, Bumpkin?'

'It hurt. The toast was hot.'

The baby girl stumbled on the rug and, after the first surprise of the fall, began to cry; Martin picked her up and carried her in his arms back to the kitchen.

'See, Daddy,' said Andy. 'The toast——'

Emily had laid the children's supper on the uncovered porcelain table. There were two plates with the remains of cream-of-wheat and eggs and silver mugs that had held milk. There was also a platter of cinnamon toast, untouched except for one tooth-marked bite. Martin sniffed the bitten piece and nibbed gingerly. Then he put the toast into the garbage pail. 'Hoo-phui—What on earth!'

Emily had mistaken the tin of cayenne for the cinnamon.

'I like to have burnt up,' Andy said. 'Drank water and ran outdoors and opened my mouth. Marianne didn't eat none.'

'Any,' corrected Martin. He stood helpless, looking around the walls of the kitchen. 'Well, that's that, I guess,' he said finally. 'Where is your mother now?'

'She's up in you alls' room.'

Martin left the children in the kitchen and went up to his wife. Outside the door he waited for a moment to still his anger. He did not knock and once inside the room he closed the door behind him.

Emily sat in the rocking chair by the window of the pleasant room. She had been drinking something from a tumbler and as he entered she put the glass hurriedly on the floor behind the chair. In her attitude there was confusion and guilt which she tried to hide by a show of spurious vivacity.

'Oh, Marty! You home already? The time slipped up on me. I was just going down——' She lurched to him and her kiss was strong with sherry. When he stood unresponsive she stepped back a pace and giggled nervously.

'What's the matter with you? Standing there like a barber pole. Is anything wrong with you?'

'Wrong with *me*?' Martin bent over the rocking chair and picked up the tumbler from the floor. 'If you could only realize how sick I am—how bad it is for all of us.'

Emily spoke in a false, airy voice that had become too familiar to him. Often at such times she affected a slight English accent, copying perhaps some actress she ad-

131

mired. 'I haven't the vaguest idea what you mean. Unless you are referring to the glass I used for a spot of sherry. I had a finger of sherry—maybe two. But what is the crime in that, pray tell me? I'm quite all right. Quite all right.'

'So anyone can see.'

As she went into the bathroom Emily walked with careful gravity. She turned on the cold water and dashed some on her face with her cupped hands, then patted herself dry with the corner of a bath towel. Her face was delicately featured and young, unblemished.

'I was just going down to make dinner.' She tottered and balanced herself by holding to the door frame.

'I'll take care of dinner. You stay up here. I'll bring it up.'

'I'll do nothing of the sort. Why, whoever heard of such a thing?'

'Please,' Martin said.

'Leave me alone. I'm quite all right. I was just on the way down——'

'Mind what I say.'

'Mind your grandmother.'

She lurched toward the door, but Martin caught her by the arm. 'I don't want the children to see you in this condition. Be reasonable.'

'Condition!' Emily jerked her arm. Her voice rose angrily. 'Why, because I drink a couple of sherries in the afternoon you're trying to make me out a drunkard. Condition! Why, I don't even touch whiskey. As well you know. *I* don't swill liquor at bars. And that's more than you can say. I don't even have a cocktail at dinnertime. I only sometimes have a glass of sherry. What, I ask you, is the disgrace of that? Condition!'

Martin sought words to calm his wife. 'We'll have a quiet supper by ourselves up here. That's a good girl.' Emily sat on the side of the bed and he opened the door for a quick departure. 'I'll be back in a jiffy.'

As he busied himself with the dinner downstairs he was lost in the familiar question as to how this problem had come upon his home. He himself had always enjoyed a good drink. When they were still living in Alabama they had served long drinks or cocktails as a matter of course. For years they had drunk one or two—possibly three drinks before dinner, and at bedtime a long nightcap. Evenings before holidays they might get a buzz on, might even become a little tight. But alcohol had never seemed a problem to him, only a bothersome expense that with the increase in the family they could scarcely afford. It was only after his company had transferred him to New York that Martin was aware that certainly his wife was drinking too much. She was tippling, he noticed, during the day.

The problem acknowledged, he tried to analyze the source. The change from Alabama to New York had somehow disturbed her; accustomed to the idle warmth of a small Southern town, the matrix of the family and cousinship and childhood friends, she had failed to accommodate herself to the stricter, lonelier mores of the North. The duties of motherhood and housekeeping were onerous to her. Homesick for Paris City, she had made no friends in the suburban town. She read only magazines and murder books. Her interior life was insufficient without the artifice of alcohol. The revelations of incontinence insidiously undermined his previous conceptions of his wife. There were times of unexplainable malevolence, times when the alcoholic fuse caused an explosion of unseemly anger. He encountered a latent coarseness in Emily, inconsistent with her natural simplicity. She lied about drinking and deceived him with unsuspected stratagems.

Then there was an accident. Coming home from work one evening about a year ago, he was greeted with screams from the children's room. He found Emily holding the baby, wet and naked from her bath. The baby had been dropped, her frail, frail skull striking the table edge, so that a thread of blood was soaking into the gossamer hair. Emily was sobbing and intoxicated. As Martin cradled the hurt child, so infinitely precious at that moment, he had an affrighted vision of the future.

The next day Marianne was all right. Emily vowed that never again would she touch liquor, and for a few weeks she was sober, cold and downcast. Then gradually she began—not whisky or gin—but quantities of beer, or sherry, or outlandish liqueurs; once he had come across a hatbox of empty crême de menthe bottles. Martin found a dependable maid who managed the household competently. Virgie was also from Alabama and Martin had never dared tell Emily the wage scale customary in New York. Emily's drinking was entirely secret now, done before he reached the house. Usually the effects were almost imperceptible—a looseness of movement or the heavy-lidded eyes. The times of irresponsibilities, such as the cayenne-pepper toast, were rare, and Martin could dismiss his worries when Virgie was at the house. But, nevertheless, anxiety was always latent, a threat of indefined disaster that underlay his days.

'Marianne!' Martin called, for even the recollection of that time brought the need for reassurance. The baby girl, no longer hurt, but no less precious to her father, came into the kitchen with her brother. Martin went on with the preparations for the meal. He opened a can of soup and put two chops in the frying pan. Then he sat down by the table and took his Marianne on his knees for a pony ride. Andy watched them, his fingers wobbling the tooth that had been loose all that week.

'Andy-the-candyman!' Martin said. 'Is that old critter still in your mouth? Come closer, let Daddy have a look.'

'I got a string to pull it with.' The child brought from his pocket a tangled thread. 'Virgie said to tie it to the tooth and tie the other end of the doorknob and shut the door real suddenly.'

Martin took out a clean handkerchief and felt the loose tooth carefully. 'That tooth is coming out of my Andy's mouth tonight. Otherwise I'm awfully afraid we'll have a tooth tree in the family.'

'A what?'

'A tooth tree,' Martin said. 'You'll bite into something and swallow that tooth. And the tooth will take root in poor Andy's stomach and grow into a tooth tree with sharp little teeth instead of leaves.'

'Shoo, Daddy,' Andy said. But he held the tooth firmly between his grimy little thumb and forefinger. 'There ain't any tree like that. I never seen one.'

'There *isn't* any tree like that and I never *saw* one.'

Martin tensed suddenly. Emily was coming down the stairs. He listened to her fumbling footsteps, his arm embracing the little boy with dread. When Emily came into the room he saw from her movements and her sullen face that she had again been at the sherry bottle. She began to yank open drawers and set the table.

'Condition!' she said in a furry voice. 'You talk to me like that. Don't think I'll forget. I remember every dirty lie you say to me. Don't you think for a minute that I forget.'

'Emily!' he begged. 'The children——'

'The children—yes! Don't think I don't see through your dirty plots and schemes. Down here trying to turn my own children against me. Don't think I don't see and understand.'

'Emily! I beg you—please go upstairs.'

'So you can turn my children—my very own children——' Two large tears coursed rapidly down her cheeks. 'Trying to turn my little boy, my Andy, against his own mother.'

With drunken impulsiveness Emily knelt on the floor before the startled child. Her hands on his shoulders balanced her. 'Listen, my Andy—you wouldn't listen to any lies your father tells you? You wouldn't believe what he says? Listen, Andy, what was your father telling you before I came downstairs?' Uncertain, the child sought his father's face. 'Tell me. Mama wants to know.'

'About the tooth tree.'

'What?'

The child repeated the words and she echoed them

135

with unbelieving terror. 'The tooth tree!' She swayed and renewed her grasp on the child's shoulder. 'I don't know what you're talking about. But listen, Andy, Mama is all right, isn't she?' The tears were spilling down her face and Andy drew back from her, for he was afraid. Grasping the table edge, Emily stood up.

'See! You have turned my child against me.'

Marianne began to cry, and Martin took her in his arms.

'That's all right, you can take *your* child. You have always shown partiality from the very first. I don't mind, but at least you can leave me my little boy.'

Andy edged close to his father and touched his leg. 'Daddy,' he wailed.

Martin took the children to the foot of the stairs. 'Andy, you take up Marianne and Daddy will follow you in a minute.'

'But Mama?' the child asked, whispering.

'Mama will be all right. Don't worry.'

Emily was sobbing at the kitchen table, her face buried in the crook of her arm. Martin poured a cup of soup and set it before her. Her rasping sobs unnerved him; the vehemence of her emotion, irrespective of the source, touched in him a strain of tenderness. Unwillingly he laid his hand on her dark hair. 'Sit up and drink the soup.' Her face as she looked up at him was chastened and imploring. The boy's withdrawal or the touch of Martin's hand had turned the tenor of her mood.

'Ma-Martin,' she sobbed. 'I'm so ashamed.'

'Drink the soup.'

Obeying him, she drank between gasping breaths. After a second cup she allowed him to lead her up to their room. She was docile now and more restrained. He laid her nightgown on the bed and was about to leave the room when a fresh round of grief, the alcoholic tumult, came again.

'He turned away. My Andy looked at me and turned away.'

Impatience and fatigue hardened his voice, but he spoke warily. 'You forget that Andy is still a little child —he can't comprehend the meaning of such scenes.'

'Did I make a scene? Oh, Martin, did I make a scene before the children?'

Her horrified face touched and amused him against his will. 'Forget it. Put on your nightgown and go to sleep.'

'My child turned away from me. Andy looked at his mother and turned away. The children——'

She was caught in the rhythmic sorrow of alcohol. Martin withdrew from the room saying: 'For God's sake go to sleep. The children will forget by tomorrow.'

As he said this he wondered if it was true. Would the scene glide so easily from memory—or would it root in the unconscious to fester in the after-years? Martin did not know, and the last alternative sickened him. He thought of Emily, foresaw the morning-after humiliation: the shards of memory, the lucidities that glared from the obliterating darkness of shame. She would call the New York office twice—possibly three or four times. Martin anticipated his own embarrassment, wondering if the others at the office could possibly suspect. He felt that his secretary had divined the trouble long ago and that she pitied him. He suffered a moment of rebellion against his fate; he hated his wife.

Once in the children's room he closed the door and felt secure for the first time that evening. Marianne fell down on the floor, picked herself up and calling: 'Daddy, watch me,' fell again, got up, and continued the falling-calling routine. Andy sat in the child's low chair, wobbling the tooth. Martin ran the water in the tub, washed his own hands in the lavatory, and called the boy into the bathroom.

'Let's have another look at that tooth.' Martin sat on the toilet, holding Andy between his knees. The child's mouth gaped and Martin grasped the tooth. A wobble, a quick twist and the nacreous milk tooth was free. Andy's face was for the first moment split between

137

terror, astonishment, and delight. He mouthed a swallow of water and spat into the lavatory. 'Look, Daddy! It's blood. Marianne!'

Martin loved to bathe his children, loved inexpressibly the tender, naked bodies as they stood in the water so exposed. It was not fair of Emily to say that he showed partiality. As Martin soaped the delicate boy-body of his son he felt that further love would be impossible. Yet he admitted the difference in the quality of his emotions for the two children. His love for his daughter was graver, touched with a strain of melancholy, a gentleness that was akin to pain. His pet names for the little boy were the absurdities of daily inspiration—he called the little girl always Marianne, and his voice as he spoke it was a caress. Martin patted dry the fat baby stomach and the sweet little genital fold. The washed child faces were radiant as flower petals, equally loved.

'I'm putting the tooth under my pillow. I'm supposed to get a quarter.'

'What for?'

'You know, Daddy. Johnny got a quarter for his tooth.'

'Who puts the quarter there?' asked Martin. 'I used to think the fairies left it in the night. It was a dime in my day, though.'

'That's what they say in kindergarten.'

'Who does put it there?'

'Your parents,' Andy said. 'You!'

Martin was pinning the cover on Marianne's bed. His daughter was already asleep. Scarcely breathing. Martin bent over and kissed her forehead, kissed again the tiny hand that lay palm-upward, flung in slumber beside her head.

'Good night, Andy-man.'

The answer was only a drowsy murmur. After a minute Martin took out his change and slid a quarter underneath the pillow. He left a night light in the room.

As Martin prowled about the kitchen making a late meal, it occurred to him that the children had not once mentioned their mother or the scene that must have seemed to them incomprehensible. Absorbed in the instant—the tooth, the bath, the quarter—the fluid passage of child-time had borne these weightless episodes like leaves in the swift current of a shallow stream while the adult enigma was beached and forgotten on the shore. Martin thanked the Lord for that.

But his own anger, repressed and lurking, arose again. His youth was being frittered by a drunkard's waste, his very manhood subtly undermined. And the children, once the immunity of incomprehension passed—what would it be like in a year or so? With his elbows on the table he ate his food brutishly, untasting. There was no hiding the truth—soon there would be gossip in the office and in the town; his wife was a dissolute woman. Dissolute. And he and his children were bound to a future of degradation and slow ruin.

Martin pushed away from the table and stalked into the living room. He followed the lines of a book with his eyes but his mind conjured miserable images: he saw his children drowned in the river, his wife a disgrace on the public street. By bedtime the dull, hard anger was like a weight upon his chest and his feet dragged as he climbed the stairs.

The room was dark except for the shafting light from the half-opened bathroom door. Martin undressed quietly. Little by little, mysteriously, there came in him a change. His wife was asleep, her peaceful respiration sounding gently in the room. Her high-heeled shoes with the carelessly dropped stockings made to him a mute appeal. Her underclothes were flung in disorder on the chair. Martin picked up the girdle and the soft, silk brassière and stood for a moment with them in his hands. For the first time that evening he looked at his wife. His eyes rested on the sweet forehead, the arch of the fine brow. The brow had descended to Marianne, and the tilt at the end of the delicate nose. In his son he could trace the high cheekbones and pointed chin. Her body was full-bosomed, slender and undulant. As

Martin watched the tranquil slumber of his wife the ghost of the old anger vanished. All thoughts of blame or blemish were distant from him now. Martin put out the bathroom light and raised the window. Careful not to awaken Emily he slid into the bed. By moonlight he watched his wife for the last time. His hand sought the adjacent flesh and sorrow paralleled desire in the immense complexity of love.

A Tree, A Rock, A Cloud

A Tree, A Rock, A Cloud

IT WAS RAINING that morning, and still very dark. When the boy reached the streetcar café he had almost finished his route and he went in for a cup of coffee. The place was an all-night café owned by a bitter and stingy man called Leo. After the raw, empty street, the café seemed friendly and bright: along the counter there were a couple of soldiers, three spinners from the cotton mill, and in a corner a man who sat hunched over with his nose and half his face down in a beer mug. The boy wore a helmet such as aviators wear. When he went into the café he unbuckled the chin strap and raised the right flap up over his pink little ear; often as he drank his coffee someone would speak to him in a friendly way. But this morning Leo did not look into his face and none of the men were talking. He paid and was leaving the café when a voice called out to him:

'Son! Hey Son!'

He turned back and the man in the corner was crooking his finger and nodding to him. He had brought his face out of the beer mug and he seemed suddenly very happy. The man was long and pale, with a big nose and faded orange hair.

'Hey Son!'

The boy went toward him. He was an undersized boy of about twelve, with one shoulder drawn higher than the other because of the weight of the paper sack. His face was shallow, freckled, and his eyes were round child eyes.

'Yeah Mister?'

The man laid one hand on the paper boy's shoulders, then grasped the boy's chin and turned his face slowly from one side to the other. The boy shrank back uneasily.

'Say! What's the big idea?'

The boy's voice was shrill; inside the café it was suddenly very quiet.

The man said slowly. 'I love you.'

All along the counter the men laughed. The boy, who had scowled and sidled away, did not know what to do. He looked over the counter at Leo, and Leo watched him with a weary, brittle jeer. The boy tried to laugh also. But the man was serious and sad.

'I did not mean to tease you, Son,' he said. 'Sit down and have a beer with me. There is something I have to explain.'

Cautiously, out of the corner of his eye, the paper boy questioned the men along the counter to see what he should do. But they had gone back to their beer or their breakfast and did not notice him. Leo put a cup of coffee on the counter and a little jug of cream.

'He is a minor,' Leo said.

The paper boy slid himself up onto the stool. His ear beneath the upturned flap of the helmet was very small and red. The man was nodding at him soberly. 'It is important,' he said. Then he reached in his hip pocket and brought out something which he held up in the palm of his hand for the boy to see.

'Look very carefully,' he said.

The boy stared, but there was nothing to look at very carefully. The man held in his big, grimy palm a photograph. It was the face of a woman, but blurred, so that only the hat and the dress she was wearing stood out clearly.

'See?' the man asked.

The boy nodded and the man placed another picture in his palm. The woman was standing on a beach in a bathing suit. The suit made her stomach very big, and that was the main thing you noticed.

'Got a good look?' He leaned over closer and finally asked: 'You ever seen her before?'

The boy sat motionless, staring slantwise at the man. 'Not so I know of.'

'Very well.' The man blew on the photographs and put them back into his pocket. 'That was my wife.'

'Dead?' the boy asked.

Slowly the man shook his head. He pursed his lips as though about to whistle and answered in a long-drawn way: 'Nuuu—' he said. 'I will explain.'

The beer on the counter before the man was in a large brown mug. He did not pick it up to drink. Instead he bent down and, putting his face over the rim, he rested there for a moment. Then with both hands he tilted the mug and sipped.

'Some night you'll go to sleep with your big nose in a mug and drown,' said Leo. 'Prominent transient drowns in beer. That would be a cute death.'

The paper boy tried to signal to Leo. While the man was not looking he screwed up his face and worked his mouth to question soundlessly: 'Drunk?' But Leo only raised his eyebrows and turned away to put some pink strips of bacon on the grill. The man pushed the mug away from him, straightened himself, and folded his loose crooked hands on the counter. His face was sad as he looked at the paper boy. He did not blink, but from time to time the lids closed down with delicate gravity over his pale green eyes. It was nearing dawn and the boy shifted the weight of the paper sack.

'I am talking about love,' the man said. 'With me it is a science.'

The boy half slid down from the stool. But the man raised his forefinger, and there was something about him that held the boy and would not let him go away.

'Twelve years ago I married the woman in the photograph. She was my wife for one year, nine months, three days, and two nights. I loved her. Yes. . . .' He tightened his blurred, rambling voice and said again: 'I loved her. I thought also that she loved me. I was a railroad engineer. She had all home comforts and luxuries. It never crept into my brain that she was not satisfied. But do you know what happened?'

'Mgneeow!" said Leo.

The man did not take his eyes from the boy's face. 'She left me. I came in one night and the house was empty and she was gone. She left me.'

'With a fellow?' the boy asked.

Gently the man placed his palm down on the counter. 'Why naturally, Son. A woman does not run off like that alone.'

The café was quiet, the soft rain black and endless in the street outside. Leo pressed down the frying bacon with the prongs of his long fork. 'So you have been chasing the floozie for eleven years. You frazzled old rascal!'

For the first time the man glanced at Leo. 'Please don't be vulgar. Besides, I was not speaking to you.' He turned back to the boy and said in a trusting and secretive undertone. 'Let's not pay any attention to him. O.K.?'

The paper boy nodded doubtfully.

'It was like this,' the man continued. 'I am a person who feels many things. All my life one thing after another has impressed me. Moonlight. The leg of a pretty girl. One thing after another. But the point is that when I had enjoyed anything there was a peculiar sensation as though it was laying around loose in me. Nothing seemed to finish itself up or fit in with the other things. Women? I had my portion of them. The same. Afterwards laying around loose in me. I was a man who had never loved.'

Very slowly he closed his eyelids, and the gesture was like a curtain drawn at the end of a scene in a play. When he spoke again his voice was excited and the words came fast—the lobes of his large, loose ears seemed to tremble.

'Then I met this woman. I was fifty-one years old and she always said she was thirty. I met her at a filling station and we were married within three days. And do you know what it was like? I just can't tell you. All I had ever felt was gathered together around this woman. Nothing lay around loose in me any more but was finished up by her.'

The man stopped suddenly and stroked his long nose. His voice sank down to a steady and reproachful undertone: 'I'm not explaining this right. What happened was this. There were these beautiful feelings and loose little pleasures inside me. And this woman was something like an assembly line for my soul. I run these little pieces of myself through her and I come out complete. Now do you follow me?'

'What was her name?' the boy asked.

'Oh,' he said. 'I called her Dodo. But that is immaterial.'

'Did you try to make her come back?'

The man did not seem to hear. 'Under the circumstances you can imagine how I felt when she left me.'

Leo took the bacon from the grill and folded two strips of it between a bun. He had a gray face, with slitted eyes, and a pinched nose saddled by faint blue shadows. One of the mill workers signaled for more coffee and Leo poured it. He did not give refills on coffee free. The spinner ate breakfast there every morning, but the better Leo knew his customers the stingier he treated them. He nibbled his own bun as though he grudged it to himself.

'And you never got hold of her again?'

The boy did not know what to think of the man, and his child's face was uncertain with mingled curiosity and doubt. He was new on the paper route; it was still strange to him to be out in the town in the black, queer early morning.

'Yes,' the man said. 'I took a number of steps to get her back. I went around trying to locate her. I went to Tulsa where she had folks. And to Mobile. I went to every town she had ever mentioned to me, and I hunted down every man she had formerly been connected with. Tulsa, Atlanta, Chicago, Cheehaw, Memphis. . . . For the better part of two years I chased around the country trying to lay hold of her.'

'But the pair of them had vanished from the face of the earth!' said Leo.

'Don't listen to him,' the man said confidentially. 'And also just forget those two years. They are not important. What matters is that around the third year a curious thing begun to happen to me.'

'What?' the boy asked.

The man leaned down and tilted his mug to take a sip of beer. But as he hovered over the mug his nostrils fluttered slightly; he sniffed the staleness of the beer and did not drink. 'Love is a curious thing to begin with. At first I thought only of getting her back. It was a kind of mania. But then as time went on I tried to remember her. But do you know what happened?'

'No,' the boy said.

'When I laid myself down on a bed and tried to think about her my mind became a blank. I couldn't see her. I would take out her pictures and look. No good. Nothing doing. A blank. Can you imagine it?'

'Say Mac!' Leo called down the counter. 'Can you imagine this bozo's mind a blank!'

Slowly, as though fanning away flies, the man waved his hand. His green eyes were concentrated and fixed on the shallow little face of the paper boy.

'But a sudden piece of glass on a sidewalk. Or a nickel tune in a music box. A shadow on a wall at night. And I would remember. It might happen in a street and I would cry or bang my head against a lamppost. You follow me?'

'A piece of glass . . .' the boy said.

'Anything. I would walk around and I had no power of how and when to remember her. You think you can put up a kind of shield. But remembering don't come to a man face forward—it corners around sideways. I was at the mercy of everything I saw and heard. Suddenly instead of me combing the countryside to find her she begun to chase me around in my very soul. *She* chasing *me,* mind you! And in my soul.'

The boy asked finally: 'What part of the country were you in then?'

'Ooh,' the man groaned. 'I was a sick mortal. It was like smallpox. I confess, Son, that I boozed. I fornicated. I committed any sin that suddenly appealed to me. I am loath to confess it but I will do so. When I recall that period it is all curdled in my mind, it was so terrible.'

The man leaned his head down and tapped his forehead on the counter. For a few seconds he stayed bowed over in this position, the back of his stringy neck covered with orange furze, his hands with their long warped fingers held palm to palm in an attitude of prayer. Then the man straightened himself; he was smiling and suddenly his face was bright and tremulous and old.

'It was in the fifth year that it happened,' he said. And with it I started my science.'

Leo's mouth jerked with a pale, quick grin. 'Well none of we boys are getting any younger,' he said. Then with sudden anger he balled up a dishcloth he was holding and threw it down hard on the floor. 'You draggle-tailed old Romeo!'

'What happened?' the boy asked.

The old man's voice was high and clear: 'Peace,' he answered.

'Huh?'

'It is hard to explain scientifically, Son,' he said. 'I guess the logical explanation is that she and I had fleed around from each other for so long that finally we just got tangled up together and lay down and quit. Peace. A queer and beautiful blankness. It was spring in Portland and the rain came every afternoon. All evening I just stayed there on my bed in the dark. And that is how the science come to me.'

The windows in the streetcar were pale blue with

light. The two soldiers paid for their beers and opened the door—one of the soldiers combed his hair and wiped off his muddy puttees before they went outside. The three mill workers bent silently over their breakfasts. Leo's clock was ticking on the wall.

'It is this. And listen carefully. I meditated on love and reasoned it out. I realized what is wrong with us. Men fall in love for the first time. And what do they fall in love with?'

The boy's soft mouth was partly open and he did not answer.

'A woman,' the old man said. 'Without science, with nothing to go by, they undertake the most dangerous and sacred experience in God's earth. They fall in love with a woman. Is that correct, Son?'

'Yeah,' the boy said faintly.

'They start at the wrong end of love. They begin at the climax. Can you wonder it is so miserable? Do you know how men should love?'

The old man reached over and grasped the boy by the collar of his leather jacket. He gave him a gentle little shake and his green eyes gazed down unblinking and grave.

'Son, do you know how love should be begun?'

The boy sat small and listening and still. Slowly he shook his head. The old man leaned closer and whispered:

'A tree. A rock. A cloud.'

It was still raining outside in the street: a mild, gray, endless rain. The mill whistle blew for the six o'clock shift and the three spinners paid and went away. There was no one in the café but Leo, the old man, and the little paper boy.

'The weather was like this in Portland,' he said. 'At the time my science was begun. I meditated and I started very cautious. I would pick up something from the street and take it home with me. I bought a goldfish and I concentrated on the goldfish and I loved it. I graduated from one thing to another. Day by day I was getting

150

this technique. On the road from Portland to San Diego——'

'Aw shut up!' screamed Leo suddenly. 'Shut up! Shut up!'

The old man still held the collar of the boy's jacket; he was trembling and his face was earnest and bright and wild. 'For six years now I have gone around by myself and built up my science. And now I am a master. Son. I can love anything. No longer do I have to think about it even. I see a street full of people and a beautiful light comes in me. I watch a bird in the sky. Or I meet a traveler on the road. Everything, Son. And anybody. All stranger and all loved! Do you realize what a science like mine can mean?'

The boy held himself stiffly, his hands curled tight around the counter edge. Finally he asked: 'Did you ever really find that lady?'

'What? What say, Son?'

'I mean,' the boy asked timidly. 'Have you fallen in love with a woman again?'

The old man loosened his grasp on the boy's collar. He turned away and for the first time his green eyes had a vague and scattered look. He lifted the mug from the counter, drank down the yellow beer. His head was shaking slowly from side to side. Then finally he answered: 'No, Son. You see that is the last step in my science. I go cautious. And I am not quite ready yet.'

'Well!' said Leo. 'Well well well!'

The old man stood in the open doorway. 'Remember,' he said. Framed there in the gray damp light of the early morning he looked shrunken and seedy and frail. But his smile was bright. 'Remember I love you,' he said with a last nod. And the door closed quietly behind him.

The boy did not speak for a long time. He pulled down the bangs on his forehead and slid his grimy little forefinger around the rim of his empty cup. Then without looking at Leo he finally asked:

'Was he drunk?'

'No,' said Leo shortly.

The boy raised his clear voice higher. 'Then was he a dope fiend?'

'No.'

The boy looked up at Leo, and his flat little face was desperate, his voice urgent and shrill. 'Was he crazy? Do you think he was a lunatic?' The paper boy's voice dropped suddenly with doubt. 'Leo? Or not?'

But Leo would not answer him. Leo had run a night café for fourteen years, and he held himself to be a critic of craziness. There were the town characters and also the transients who roamed in from the night. He knew the manias of all of them. But he did not want to satisfy the questions of the waiting child. He tightened his pale face and was silent.

So the boy pulled down the right flap of his helmet and as he turned to leave he made the only comment that seemed safe to him, the only remark that could not be laughed down and despised:

'He sure has done a lot of traveling.'